D0886920

THE BANISHMENT

BOOKS BY ALMA STONE

The Banishment
The Bible Salesman
The Harvard Tree

ALMA STONE

The Banishment

AND THREE STORIES
The Portrait
The Traveler
Oh, Pity the Dwarf's Butt

Doubleday & Company, Inc., Garden City, New York 1973

*The characters, events, and situations
depicted in this novel are creations of the
author, and any resemblance to actual persons,
events, or situations is purely accidental.*

Chapters Fifteen and Sixteen were previously
published under the title "The Street Corner
Coordinator" in the *Antioch Review,* Summer
1969. Copyright © 1969 by Antioch Press.

ISBN: 0-385-03899-2
LIBRARY OF CONGRESS CATALOG CARD NUMBER 72-92246
COPYRIGHT © 1973 BY ALMA STONE
ALL RIGHTS RESERVED
PRINTED IN THE UNITED STATES OF AMERICA
FIRST EDITION

Thank you, Janet

THE BANISHMENT

CHAPTER ONE

"The old ladies must go." It was his method to get to the point at once, often an offense to the other three members of the Committee, less hurried than he, and given to preliminary pencil pushing. "They're overrunning the city. Everywhere you go an old lady's already there or a pigeon has just been." Now the Leader, he had once been in business, passed the office-managing test, and beat an old lady out of a job. The look in her eyes the day he came to replace her still haunted him. For a long time she would not get up from her desk, locking it in a way only she knew and hiding the stamps where it took him days to locate them. He had not felt like the head at all with the old lady; he still felt as if she was the head, and until he could free himself of her memory (leaning back in the chair, laughing while he sweated and tugged at the desk) he sat like a horseless rider and rode like a spurless king.

"The city simply cannot contain or tolerate them," he said.

The other members, beyond shocking now, looked at him and said nothing. Their continued silence put him on the defensive and this, as they had planned, angered and frightened him more; a Leader on the defensive soon ceased to be the Leader. "Well, we got rid of the buildings. What they call the landmarks," he said. "And the parks. We stripped 'em of the parks. It's easy."

"There were people who objected, though," said the politician, and walked over to the window, more of a wall than a window. Using the telescope panel, he looked down, stories below, to the public terrace of the building next door. An old man on a bench was trying to get a sparrow to eat out of his hand. Nearby, under the concrete trees, old ladies were feeding the pigeons. It was their great pleasure, this giving of the bread, the feeding of the birds, even this high in the air on stone and cement, and soon when the winter came, forcing the old ladies indoors, this pleasure would be gone. But a few would make it somehow or send crumbs by younger women. One old lady, feeling the chill come on, was pinning the tops of her stockings to her drawers; every fall, just before the Harvard-Princeton game, she hitched them up like this; it kept out the draft. She looked at the girls passing: you, too, someday. The girls quickly averted their eyes: impossible, were they not young and/ or beautiful, owners of the world? This made the old lady laugh. Suddenly the old man froze into position: look, a sparrow at last eating from his hand. Day after day, try, try, try, and now at last; he held his hand very still. But the old lady, restless, moved on to the next bench; it had always been like this around game time;

4

just before the whistle blew with the mad rough-and-tumble, something inside her stirred. Startled by her movement, the sparrow flew away. The old man threw up an empty hand and smacked his forehead; shrugging then, he bent to try again.

The politician came back to his seat at the council table. "People protested, goddam it," he said. He particularly disliked the way the leader rushed them; of an expansive nature and a good raising in the South, he liked to walk around the room in a leisurely fashion, to say "Hi, Harry," "How you, Joe," before he got down to business. Put a little graciousness in it, for God's sake. "If you're going to be a son of a bitch, son," his father had told him, "be a gracious one." Like at home when he ordered his wife or his mother to "Shut up," he always added politely, "for a while." He kept it on a goddam high plane. Sometimes around election time he would add "please," strictly as a reflex, for the Committee had already got rid of that little private voting booth. (Who knew what they did when they got in there, curtains pulled, no holds barred, old scores to even? What had Mamie and Lady Bird done in those bygone days? How about Pat? And Muriel? Had their old boys ever guessed?)

"People objected about the parks," he said firmly. He liked to rustle a piece of paper when he was on a big deal like this and look around the table clockwise, as if a picture were being taken by some famous weekly maga-

5

zine. He liked it to look as if he participated. But in a picture snapped at this table only the Leader, who faced the inner door, would fully show and one member, the Yid, thought the politician, would be blocked out except for his back. Certainly he, the politician, and the jig would get in. "There were objections," he said, and would have liked to hear some minutes read from the previous meeting. He reached out to arrange his pencils, parallel. "There were people who hated to see the parks go," he said, and put a paper of matches in line with the pencils.

"How many?" said the Leader, and smiled, remembering. One of the few, elderly, intense, had thrown herself around the trunk of a tree and cried, "Thy ax shall harm it not"; they had damn near sawed the old lady in half.

"I miss the buildings," said one of the other Committee men, having in mind a certain depot, low, built along Roman lines and said to be a classic. He did not lift his eyes to meet the others'; the height of the present building made him sick but he dreaded to rise and go to the men's room where, nudging the clouds, the toilets flushed like those of airplanes, unnerving with their septic mystery. If he kept looking down, his mouth open to one side, and went ssz, ssz, ssz like a man with a plastic esophagus, he noticed the height less; also he did not have to look at the Leader, directly across the table from him. Sometimes, to get away from heights, he had gone to the station just to go ssz, ssz unnoticed in a corner of the

6

waiting room, and to wonder how long the trains, getting shorter and shorter, would continue to come in. Each time a train was cut down, sold to the minors, or slipped quietly out of service, he felt the ssz, ssz increase. One old train, bucking the system, kept backing up, hating to go, knowing it was the end, yet unable to understand it. (How explain to a train that it was through?) Riding the wrong tracks, blowing the wrong whistle, beating another train into the station, it had caused a hell of a ruckus. Kill it, kill it, said irate people, left stranded for hours, or spending the night at a gyp hotel in a city they had never meant to visit. Oh yeah, somebody must have been at the throttle, they said. A person, they bet.

"I miss the station very much."

"You mean you miss the hot, putrid air on a summer day when the jigaboos go through," said the Leader, then remembered the Negro member sitting to his left, and stopped, though not apologizing. The black man sat silent, enduring the slip he had hoped was not inevitable; at home he had foolishly said so: "It will not happen, we are past that; if nothing else, they are scared as hell." But the politician, outraged, said quickly, to change the subject, "I know some very fine old ladies." One should not talk that way about Nigras, in front of them, he thought; this was never done Down Home in the best families, and not often now even in the worst. Even way back there, working in the Food Distributing Office dur-

ing the depression, he had called them Nigra. Each dis-
patch of food had had his personal attention with a note.

"Why pick on the old ladies?" he asked the Leader.
"Why not pick on the lousy youth, the so-called Leaders
of tomorrow?"

A Leader does not answer questions (a Leader who
answered questions was soon asking them again) and he
looked at the politician, on his right, to so remind him,
almost gentle with this fatuous fool. Uneasy, the politician said, "Don't look at me like that. I've banned some of
the goddamnedest best things in this city. Remember how
they used to have free concerts? Who put a stop to that?
How about the flower planting in the esplanades? Who
got rid of that? My record speaks for itself. But I got nothing against old ladies, for Pete's sake. In fact I remember
one with great fondness. Miss Emma. She lived on the
same street we did in this cute little old southern town
and one day I went to her house and said, 'Miss Emma,
I smell teacakes.' 'You do, G.W.?' she said, and then,
laughing, she got 'em down off the shelf. Her own kids
were all grown and she was tickled to death I paid her
this attention." He glanced around the table. "Look 'em
in the face," said his father, "stare 'em down, you're as
real a legitimate bastard as any of 'em." Daring the
Leader now ("It's printed right on your birth certificate,
son: R.L.B."), he laid a piece of paper on the table before

8

him—minutes of the last meeting, by God, taken on the sly.

The Negro, distracted a moment by this daring procedure, took his gaze from the inner door, then, suspecting some trick, returned to his vigil. When he saw the door open he meant to rise and stand in front of the camera, obliterating the view of the others. His idea now was to be the whole thing, though at first this had not been his idea; at first he had meant to share. The others looked at him, guessing his intent.

"Why do we not then change the voting law," said the Leader, who when seemingly asking a question never put in the question mark and whenever he remembered never said "don't" or "can't"; he said "do not" and "cannot" or put the "not" way down near the verb, classy. "Nobody over fifty-five can vote. Women, that is."

The others eyed the politician: Farewell, Miss Emma, Old Teacake Mixer, Miss Dixie Doodle. He put the pencils in line neatly again before he said, "When you finalize it, the old lady was tricky as hell, letting me think I'd pulled a fast one, smelling the teacakes. And as the years passed and she couldn't see to bake, but just so she could laugh and feel good, I still asked for those lousy teacakes I had to throw away later. 'Do it though, son,' my father said, 'do it graciously, take the goddamned teacakes from the old faker.' Often she put salt in them instead of sugar. I wonder now if maybe she didn't do it on purpose, if

9

maybe that's what she was laughing at." He moved the minutes in line with the pencils and the matches; the perfidy of the old lady made his hands tremble. Yet he was determined to be magnanimous. Very severe again, he looked around the table, the way he had when the subject of the parks first came up: absolutely no. Or maybe just one little old Nigra or Porto park, in the bad part of town where it wouldn't show or be missed. "But naturally I couldn't consent to seeing old ladies like Miss Emma go." Deliberately he rattled the piece of paper and, in the guise of crossing his legs, angled his chair for a better view of the inner door.

"All right then, we get rid of the old Jewish ladies first," said the Leader, and the Committee men nodded wisely, except Mr. Gottlieb, who had seen it coming again. Watching it come again, he had grown old and heavy, train-crazy and scared of heights, a man who in the corners of waiting rooms went ssz, ssz like his Aunt Etta from Warsaw. In the ghetto one day they had beaten Aunt Etta who, defying the ban, was looking for her husband, Uncle Zolly, already dead. When she had come to this country he remembered walking with the strange woman who had to stop, dizzy, on the streets and breathe ssz, ssz, ssz. When people looked at them curiously, the plump boy trailing the afflicted woman, he had tried to pretend he was not with her, that he was mathematical, a great chess player figuring something out, the reason he walked so slowly and behind. At the same time he tried to make Aunt Etta think that he was with her. (I am with you, Aunt Etta, I *am*.) But he had sensed that the woman, old at forty, bent, breathing with difficulty, knew his duplicity.

"No discrimination," he said faintly, and the dizziness came over him again. His head bowed. Often, it was reported, he would sit in his office and not ban a thing all day. Some said he read; others did not go this far, for he was still honored by many from his university days; they merely said he was in poor health. Unsympathetic, the Committee men turned on him now: why the hell hadn't they stood up to Hitler instead of blaming it all on the Pope, why hadn't they shown some guts? "They all go the same way, the same time," he roused himself to say briskly. With this effort, the volume of the ssz, ssz rose.

"That's right," said the Negro and, mistaking the keening sound of the ssz, ssz for the opening of the door, stood. The others gazed at him, half hiding their smiles. Ready to stand up now, are you? Why not before? What were you and old Mandy doing back there in the kitchen together so long? Fucking? A hundred years? "No discriminating unless I do it," said the Negro. He sat back down, looked at the door, and got ready. "I have first right to all discrimination."

"I couldn't have smelled the goddam teacakes," said the politician. "She had 'em away up in a jar on the shelf where she kept the coon cheese. I mean rat," he said, flustered, and again straightened the pencils and paper.

The Negro smiled grimly, kept gazing at the door, and waited.

"Of course, no discriminating—" said the Leader, and stiffened into silence. Outside the glass-walled building, wings fluttered and disappeared. The members gazed at one another, refusing to believe it. Sixty stories below, possibly, but not up here. It had been in the contract: no bird or old lady this high: forbidden.

The pigeon returned and tried to land on the sill-less ledge. Almost afraid now, the Committee members watched it. Only the Negro, wary, kept his back to the window and his eyes focused on the inner door. The pigeon tried to cling to the cold glass, then, falling, moaning, flew off, but in a moment was back, slamming its golden-brown feathers against the glass. The Negro kept his eyes trained on the inner door; the politician and Mr. Gottlieb rushed to the window. Stories below, on the terrace, an old lady shook her keys, picked up the stunned bird, and put it in her shopping bag.

The Leader had remained seated; Leaders did not rush to windows—but once. "We will start with the pigeons," he said.

"Oh yes, by association," said the others. Dazzled again by his genius, they looked up to him, still their Leader. Suddenly his right hand swept the table clear of the pencils and paper, the way he had tried it on the old

lady. But she had kept sitting at the locked desk, in pos-
session, with no one inclined to help dislodge her except
Security, who had bodily removed her. "Jesus, what an
artist!" said the locksmith when he came. "Who the hell
made the key to this lock, buddy? Look at them interstices, honed like fine grillwork, man."

Gazing at the broken lock, at the intricate key secreted
in the drawer, the Leader had known he would one day
find a way. "What you got your desk drawers loaded
with all this pigeon food for, buddy? You one of them
pigeon nuts?" Dumping the seed down the john, he had
known he would find a way to get rid of her forever.
Ordinarily answering emergency calls for clogged johns
the plumber did not intrude. He figured so what? That's
their business. But this time he had felt compelled. "Somebody's in trouble here," he'd said. "Somebody's sick."

"Gottlieb is sick," said the Leader now. "Poor Gottlieb
is choking to death from the bird. We must get rid of the
birds." And now he threw back his head, smiling, little
king. From the inner room, the door opened and a bulb
flashed. Caught by surprise, the politician, stooping to
pick up his pencils and paper, seemed to be kneeling in
adoration at the Leader's feet. Mr. Gottlieb, terrified by
the *ssz ssz* sound that came from his doomed throat,
staggered to his feet. Lurching toward the men's room,
he shut from view the Negro who had risen, too late, for
the snap of the camera.

Slowly the Negro followed the others to the elevator.

He hated to go home and tell it again—that even in the banishment of the old ladies they had got ahead of him, beaten by the same old Jew, the same old Whiteys. Still so very much to learn from them, he thought, almost admiringly, so very much. But he would, he knew he would.

CHAPTER TWO

The afternoon papers carried a headline, "Committee Bans Pigeons," and the radio and TV picked it up for special evening coverage, as they had for the landmarks and the parks. By night all the old ladies in the city had been alerted. At the end of three days an underground was in operation.

"We are under siege," wrote Miss Sarah Adams in bright red Crayola. "Our tentative and sporadic support —students spouting Hegel and Marx, boys who raise pigeons and perhaps even an old lady or two on rooftops, eating-counter proprietors who go boldly to the culvert and, calling the pigeons 'pals,' feed them hard rolls—has evaporated. Groups that used to phone each day to see if we were all right, or come by to shop for us, have had to quit. The Unitarian Church, the Civil Liberties Union, the Window Washers of America, Mom, organizations from which we would have been assured aid in a less totalitarian regime, have worked vainly in our behalf. Women's Liberation, which toiled the hardest and longest for us, marching and picketing, organizing groups and workshops, urging us to unite, to vote, to protest, teaching us to be our own doctors, to see our own cervix,

17

to reduce our menstrual flow, has finally yielded to the demands of the Committee. Division in its ranks, possible infiltration by government spies, and the temptation, it is rumored, to later rid itself of some of its older, more vociferous leaders, were the apparent causes of its unwilling capitulation.

"We are, as we had foreseen, on our own. Citizens who previously spoke to us now walk on the other side of the street and do not wish to be involved or seen in our company. 'Pigeon feeder, pigeon lover' are names whispered around. And the old men, our contemporaries of the opposite sex, what have they done to help? Nothing. They are scared to peep. But have not many of us been through all this before, alone?" And exchanging the Crayola for another, she smiled: how could you be lonely, with your life history on the wall and a pigeon in your room?

Defying the ban, the old ladies continued to take home the young, the sick, and the crippled birds and hide them in their rented rooms. When the police came they would go quietly, barely tap, tap, tapping the warning to the room next door. Listening behind the wall, another old lady would whisper, "Softer, softer," to the fluttering pigeon on the nest of frayed sweaters.

"The ban has given license to cruelty," wrote Sarah in deep purple over the sink.

On the sidewalks dead pigeons were found, wings folded under, heads twisted sideways, necks broken. But the old ladies gathered up the birds in their shopping bags and, scratching in the parks, now called concretes, tried to bury them, covering them with box tops and leaving something, a button, a defunct trading stamp, for remembrance. After this was forbidden, too, the old ladies, racked with memories, recalling how it had been in other cities in other times of the pursued, the unwanted, sat up late in the rented rooms, shades drawn, composing letters to the press. "It is the familiar pattern of oppression. Remember that Greek play where the leader, Cleon Jones, will not let the girl, Antig-a-ma-jig, bury her brother, what's-his-name?" wrote Sarah, forgetful of names and places in these full and frightful times.

They are dirty, useless, destructive, said the Committee members, they have caused death to our great citizen, Mr. Gottlieb, and others. And on the wall Sarah noted that the order did not say "pigeons" any more, but "they." Perhaps a few birds did carry disease, the old ladies granted in conclave, adding quickly, "even as you and I." Many of them had some distressing minor ailment, coughing at night, dizziness when they looked up suddenly, inability to concentrate when people spoke right at them. (Sometimes when people stood close to them and talked right at them it drove everything out of their minds completely, or set them to thinking on something entirely different that had happened some time ago, or even in another country.) "We are very sorry to hear people died," said the old ladies, who hated to see anything die. "We are grieved that Mr. Gottlieb is no longer with us, dying unexpectedly in that dark alley of asphyxiation and immediately replaced on the Committee by Mr. Mamamia, our other required ethnic representative. But poisonous fumes have never come up from droppings and killed *us*," they said, answering the Committee's charge.

"Anyway, it is no reason to destroy a whole flock," said the old ladies. "And what of the gifted ones," they asked, "those proven capable of precision pecking in the factories and laboratories?" "Let 'em get their own union," said the local, "they're taking people's jobs." "The bearers of messages then, the carrier pigeons?" they asked. "What they gonna carry now, lady?" was the answer. "They gonna carry the bomb now, lady?"

But the old ladies could not be stilled. Scurrying about the city, slipping in and out of back doors, circulating petitions, passing out more leaflets, they put on the steam. Some who had never cared for pigeons before, often shooing them in a disrespectful manner and ranking them with roaches, came to champion their cause. "It is not just the pigeons. Gradually they will extend the ban to everything connected with pigeons. Next it will be you. They will not be able to tell a flock of old ladies from a flock of pigeons." This is what the old ladies, reckless now in their extremity, wrote in the leaflets.

"Oh, for goodness' sakes, did you ever hear anything so silly?" said people who formerly had stood up for the old ladies and admired their spunk. "We can tell a flock of pigeons from a flock of old ladies easy. The pigeons have feathers, and don't carry shopping bags." It was rather touching, though, they said; the old ladies didn't really give a damn about the pigeons; an attention-getting device was all it was. Old ladies had become like children. Amused, they looked forward to what ridiculous thing the old ladies would say next, and there grew up in the city what were called Old Lady Watchers. Every afternoon two old ladies would stand across the street from each other and wave their canes. Sometimes people stopped to watch a minute before they walked on, nearly smiling. It became a kind of club, meeting to ask, "Did the old ladies wave today? What did the old ladies say funny today?"

One old lady, caught feeding pigeons, tried to shoo them away, to pretend she did not know them, that she was on some strange, other mission that made her bend her back and throw out handfuls of birdseed. A witch or a great scientist was most likely what she was. But the pigeons, unable to mask their greedy joy at seeing her, unwilling to dissemble, to deny her in public, swarmed at her feet. "The pigeons are perhaps *eating*, but I am *feeding* the *sparrows*," she said, cornered. "The moral quality of any action lies in its intention." This, a precept learned long ago in college, she firmly believed, but another one, the feather and the hammer falling at the same velocity, she'd never been able to swallow. Now, her skin wrinkled like tripe, her old hands turned out toward the birds, on one arthritic finger one solitaire diamond (her engagement ring and the only thing left from home except Mama's pearl-handled knives and forks, pretty well cracked now but hidden when Welfare came to check), she went quietly. "I just frankly don't think it's possible," she told the policeman. "But I shall keep trying the experiment of course. I never give up on experiments."

"Hell, yes, I feed everything hungry," said another, Anna Maria Wychokovski. And she ran after pigeon detractors yelling, "Scum of America. Have *you* quit eating?"

This one was really putting on a good show, people said. Why buy expensive tickets to a no-good Broadway play when you could see this old actress free? Playing it like theater then, the old ladies sat on the standpipes and wooden boxes in front of supermarkets and fruit stands and sunned. Box seats for the Broadway show. Using a stitch called "throw over, go in twice" or simply "suet," they crocheted the tiny bags for the winter days when they would hang fat for the birds from the concrete trees. If the fire engines clanged the old ladies, barely dropping a stitch, got off the standpipes and watched the firemen attach the big hose. When the water had roared through the hose and the firemen, successful, departed, the old ladies, like old queens on private thrones, ascended the pipes again.

They searched the garbage cans as they had customarily done, though it now seemed that they chose more selectively, weighing the objects in their hands, estimating, like a thrower. "Umbrella handles, broken bricks, toy guns, empty bottles, are especially good," wrote Sarah on the wall. People watched them and treated it as a joke, but some, taking a more serious view, said, "Keep your mother in tonight." A law that all shopping bags were to be searched, then rationed, only one to each old lady, was passed by the Committee.

"Some of us, of course, are afraid to go out at night," wrote Sarah. "Many of us have been victims of the mugger; we have been relieved when the first mugging, overdue, has occurred, so we can relax till the next one. Some of us have died at the merciless hands of the crazed dope addict. But this has happened not only on the street but in our rooms as well.

"Old ladies, like persecuted races, do not survive by fear, by holing up in horror, three locks on the door. We will never concede that this is the *only* way we can survive. We do not accept death as the answer to poverty-stricken, oppressed old age. Old ladies survive by daring to face the danger. In our case, the danger from our government and our so-called friends exceeds the danger from the street.

"So most of us continue to go out at night, search the garbage cans, or sit on the standpipes and wooden boxes. All other places where we could sit or pigeons could

THE BANISHMENT

roost have been destroyed," wrote Sarah. "The small
buildings, the statues, the fountains, the benches are
gone. But no one dares to get rid of the standpipes.

"Perhaps at this point in our history an explanatory
note should be interposed for those unfamiliar with the
purpose and form of the standpipes. These are the con-
nections and junctures, usually jutting from the wall of a
building, but sometimes standing free, that link the water
connection of that building with the fire department or
the sprinkler system. Approximately six inches in diam-
eter, many are single, and if two in number, are called
Siamese and are more comfortable. Of varying heights,
none taller than two to three feet, they are not to be confused with the larger, vertical cistern pipe or tower of
the same name used by homeowners, or with the sprinkler valve. Their attraction to older ladies is their ac-
cessibility (the sprinkler valve may be behind a grating),
sturdy construction, and flat surface.

"They are usually painted red.

"When these are all occupied we stand on the street
and lean against the walls of buildings. We talk softly
or stare straight ahead. If we are arrested, the jail doors
are instantly opened. How fortunate," she added, "that
I have this real knack for making keys, learned at night
school when I realized that squirt, the new Leader,
would come to take my place."

Coming home from a meeting one evening, the Leader
tripped and fell; an old lady with a cane quickly entered

the cafeteria. When he followed her inside he found her indistinguishable from the multitude of others staring at him from the tables. "With our canes and our crutches, we managed to appear most forbidding," wrote Sarah. "Like old hawks, ready to strike." Cafeterias were dangerous, decided the Leader, and had them closed. The next day when he was on his way to the Tower Room, a potted plant smashed at his feet. "So now it is flowers. No more flowers. What next?" wondered Sarah.

"The old ladies," said the Leader. "They must be registered and numbered and banished."

"And it is this ass," wrote Sarah, "whom they chose to succeed me, whom they allowed to take my desk and my job from me. What will they say now?"

"Why, we're just as shocked as can be," said the people. "We'll never agree that old ladies be banished. Why, some of our best—" In private they told one another, "'Save her, save her,' he said to me, 'she's my mother, it don't look so good we don't save her.' 'Sure,' I said, 'do not crush the old lady, let the old lady crush you. Frankly,' I said, 'an old lady will suck your life's blood, then look around for a chaser.'" Young women, safe in their youth, said nothing. But a few older girls said, "Now see here, just a minute. Hadn't we better consider this further?" There they themselves had been, young as could be, and all of a sudden when they'd looked around they were these middle-aged women. Who had seen it happen—the slack in the neckline, the first white hair in

25

the crotch? "Of course we'll not hear to banishing the old ladies—yet," they said. "However, we don't see how it will hurt them to be registered and numbered. Actually it's for their own good, what you call a protection. If anything happens to them you know who they are. See what we mean?"

CHAPTER THREE

"So we saw what they meant," wrote Sarah, using muted gray. "Patiently, almost like idiots, we waited in long lines to be registered and numbered. We were not all nutty and we were not all sane. Some were freaks, some were not. Some may have had unusual avocations—car building, hammer throwing. Key making might even be considered in that category. But the only things many had in common were that they were women, no longer young, and unwanted. This does not mean that some in late life had not been loved and cared for. It means only that such ladies were the exception, that they had been paying their own way or had had unmarried daughters who, in need of lives of their own to live, had given all. But even these old ladies did not escape.

"Lumped together in the line-up, former executive, professional Little Old Lady, slack wearer, granny dress-er, bourbon drinker, teetotaler, atheist, religious fanatic, we were soon all acting alike. Some of the things we did were ridiculous, but we were not funny. We laughed at ourselves, but it was no joke. A few of us fainted or pretended to; revived, these were given priority in line. Resentment flared among the ranks at this preferential treatment and many began to feign faints. We stood close to one another then, as in a supermarket, and would not allow our places in line to be taken."

There were incidents on the street; shoved, the old ladies shoved back. There was shouting. "Why don't you go back where you came from?" People met in groups and said, "Did you hear what they did in the subway, how they frightened the passengers? Did you see how they are ripping up the subway seats and splashing the walls with paint? Have you seen the names and numbers they are using, as though it were someone else—Joe 138, Crazy Cross De Cita 254? Did you know that even in the station that is closed they have crawled in the dark up the tracks and sprayed on the name and the number, Tony 506, Kotex 134? Nah, of course they don't get electrocuted. They're too tricky and sly. Ever hear of an old bag getting electrocuted on the third rail?"

When one old lady, feeding a stray dog at night, fell in a pothole in the street and others came to her rescue, it was reported that they were out to capture the city. Barricades had been thrown up in the Con Edison ditches, it was said, and manned by old ladies. Recruits, it was rumored, were pouring into the city over the George Washington Bridge. Some had been killed in the traffic.

Other reinforcements, storming down from upstate, had captured the toll stations, collecting enough money in one hour to finance their campaign all winter. Excited by hearsay, people got in their cars and drove out, taking the children, who had never been to a real war yet, to see the carnage. But the report on TV was false; a new announcer, hoping for a higher rating, had invented it. Only one old lady, it turned out, had been wounded; chasing her lost cat across the bridge, she had been scratched by the frightened animal. Driving back to the city, people called it a flop, another damn TV commercial flop, and they remarked on the new housing development going up. It was one they had not noticed before, tall and thick, right on the edge of the city, almost like a wall, they said.

"You see how dangerous the old ladies are," said the Committee, and where there had once been talk of Black Power there was now fear of Old Lady Power. Institutionalized racism became old ladyism. And now the old ladies, long-nosed, iron-faced, were fighting for their very freedom. Now it was said that the cane wavers, deemed so innocent once, were using a signal.

"They got Tippy today," wrote Sarah in black crayon. "She and I stood on opposite sides of the street and waved as we have done for years. It's cheaper than telephoning. Three fingers up mean 'Meet you at Schrafft's as usual.' Thumb down: 'Can't go today, make it tomorrow instead,' and we make a T with two fingers. Today, a crowd, suspicious, soon gathered. They looked so silly there, waiting to pounce on poor old Tippy and me, that we could not forgo a joke. I held up my hand, four fingers showing, and ticked them off—off with the heads of the four Committee members. The *T* I made today I tried to make look like a guillotine, at least as much as I remembered it from that nice Ronald Colman and the French Revolution. To cap my point I made that little gesture across the throat.

"Tippy gave back the old hockey victory salute we had in prep school. Cane high above her head, she looked daring and glorious, as she always did on the field. 'Get her, get her,' cried the crowd, and on orders from the Leader, they quickly closed in. By darting into an illegal cafeteria, operated as an OTB parlor, I was able to escape. But Tippy, even with her arthritis, could not resist trying for a final goal—On, Medford, ever on—and they got her. But they did not take her alive.

"Now I must pack my things, my books—Shakespeare, Hawthorne, Melville, Dewey, *Goodbye, Mr. Chips*—and the wounded pigeon, Honey. And of course, the key machine, heavy. A persuasive little girl, quite enterprising for her age—knows how to get Crayolas free—has induced an acquaintance of hers to haul it for her. Though a rather rough fellow, he seemed quite submissive to the little girl.

"And now I must go to our underground hideaway. My writing henceforth will mostly be confined to harassment leaflets, as the walls there are covered with pipes.

"But I will return. After all, what is new about the present banishment? Have we not been ostracized, banished for years? What of those in the nursing homes, the old ladies in the TV rooms staring silently at the screen or standing in the hopeless halls, trailing their urine bags, sentenced for life? ("I'm so sad I could cry my eyes out. People have to help me to pee.") What of those who have chosen alcoholism and suicide rather than living death? Is this not banishment? Is it worse than ours?

"Let us see."

CHAPTER FOUR

Some people, Communists, hid the old ladies in attics and basements. They found some, seeking refuge, slumped against the wall, like sick old pigeons who had stepped into a doorway to die. Lying on pallets on the floor, hunted, haunted, besieged, the old ladies would practice dying, letting their tongues roll out of their mouths and their eyes grow glazed. Or they would prop up their arms stiffly on the floor, at a right angle, the only old ladies ever to die in that city with their arms propped so. (Usually they were lying flat, or slung out over the bed, the old body maybe even knifed or raped.) Some would cry out in terror and others comforted them in the night. Some, rising stealthily from their beds, would creep out into the city with their canes and crutches and umbrellas. And one night, coming home, the Leader was attacked and badly beaten.

The next day all the old ladies of the city were routed out of their hiding places. Those from the streets were taken first. Living out of their shopping bags, sleeping on somebody's floor or fleabag at night, but turned out on the street early each morning, these old ladies were easy game. Others were harder to find. One had secretly raised and hidden a little park of green. Behind a church, where no one ever came, it had been a safe gathering place for the old women. When the edict went out several of them, eating their lunches in the sun, were captured here. One tore away from her guard and went back to get her potted plant. It was old and shriveled; it needed the sun, like her. But perhaps it would bloom again somewhere. Like her. She held it high, protecting the brittle leaves.

The trigger-happy captor shot her in self-defense. The plant fell but another old lady grabbed it and fled.

Herded into a square on the edge of the city, the old ladies were assigned to buses. Some went empty-handed, as though for a day's excursion, a free trip up the river. One had dressed for the occasion, with a ribbon from a Jack Daniel gift bottle in her hair. Some who had never had a home of their own, always "yessing" some other woman, yes, yes, yes, hoped to find a new place, small, of course, probably not even with a tree or a window, or one of those used oriental rugs, but all her own. These took along things in their shopping bags—a parakeet, a sliver of sweet soap, a china cup, Limoges, no handle, an extra sweater, full of feathers but one sleeve was still good— anything that would come in handy in a new life.

They looked at one another silently: what of the animals, our pets, watching and waiting? Who could look into the eyes of a waiting pet and say no? Many tried to sneak them into the buses, dogs, cats, canaries, their yellow wings never still, but the buses were overloaded and the guards threw the animals out. Some of the ladies then sat looking straight ahead, dumped on the seats like ice. Others darted quick little looks to the right and to the left, as if to remember how it was this time. If a few prayed, it was from habit and with no longer any expectancy of divine intervention.

One spoke of her son. "I liked old Robert. I thought he liked me. Whoever thought it would end this way?" Puzzled, she sought an explanation from her seatmate. "I was very quiet and meek. I tried not to be in the way. Why did he turn me in? Why was I banished? What did I do wrong?" "You forgot to die," said her seatmate, and as was her custom on any subway or bus, she indicated empty seats to those who stood, and pushed them with her cane, sometimes catapulting them into other old ladies' laps, at which some of the old ladies giggled, but others sat dumb, or thought of better days.

One crouched on the seat, as though stripped naked. Once she had had an old sick man pulling her down, down. Seven years, then she had been set free, free to live the exciting days when she had roamed the noisy streets, with all her possessions in her shopping bags, bags with glorious, ringing names—Gimbel's East, Larry's Fish Market, Send Bella Back. She had felt like somebody then. Escaping from the tiny room early each morning, pushing her creaking shopping cart, discarded by Daitch's, through the busy streets, expertly crossing the streets against the lights—See the people jump! Hear the drivers curse!—she had been a person to cope with. Pausing in a store entrance as though choosing this for her campsite for the day, she had elicited fear and respect.

But it was not the challenge and the freedom of each day—whom shall I choose to honor with my presence today, with my blue counterpane, my bath towel, my other dress, my little stew pan, my lovely remnant of oilcloth, raveled, dirty, but mine? What store proprietors will pay me the biggest bribes today? What interesting people will I converse with?—What shall I do if it rains, if it snows? It was not these, the diversities of each day, that she would miss the most. Some old women, sitting it out behind the swollen legs and the painted cheeks, liked to watch old men, waiting for them to fail, or stumble. But she watched Broadway parking, and it was this she would miss—the dented fenders, the cursing motorists, the frequent fights for space. It was the little extra touches she liked the most; the little special something like scraping both cars, the front *and* the back one, or picking out only one taillight to bust when you could have had two. It was things like this that meant a real human being was out there parking, bothering to be a little bit creative.

From her vantage point behind the shopping cart she had seen some of the worst and some of the best parkers in the city. Young black men were best; old Chinese women, scarce, the worst. Sometimes, directing them from her shopping-bag retreat—Turn the wheel the other way, dope—she felt a kinship with them, a feeling that their problem was parallel to hers and she hoped they would make it, and sometimes, as perverse as any other old woman, she was glad when they failed. She felt that if she had been able to make it, to get where she had, with that sick old man pulling her down, down, they should too. Wasn't that what life was all about? Park and unpark? Add a little extra pizzazz?

She sighed now and slumped further on the seat by her companion. Stripped of her shopping bags, right there in front of the bank, she felt naked and insecure. She felt degraded to nothing. How would the president of the First National City Bank like to have *his* bags taken away, right in front of everybody?

Her seat companion wore her security on her person. As a kind of renown, she had on her bosom the mark of a dumpling—the three-quarter-inch size, homemade. Dishing it up, carefree and gay as was her wont on Dumpling Day, singing, *"Gnocchi, gnocchi, belli gnocchi,"* she had felt a red-hot one slip down inside her dress. A few of her neighbors, hearing her startled cry and seeing the imprint, had thought it was the stigmata, and crossed themselves in her presence. Later, in neighborhood fairs for St. Anthony, she showed the mark for charity.

All who had loved her had revered this mark, and those who kissed her bosom headed for the dumpling mark second. City-wide fame became hers; pasta products bore her endorsement (Next to Me I like Pasta Products Best), a lingerie company, in her honor, called its new brassiere the Dumpling Booster; "cut low as the dumpling" became a saying in the garment district. Some, naturally, envied her. In her native village, said one neighbor, a girl had had a much bigger mark. "Ripples. Like lasagna." This was doubted and taken for what it was, a play for prominence. "So many girls these days don't get the dumpling mark," said the younger girls, but most were satisfied with something inferior. The old lady's skin had grown cracked and leathery but the dumpling mark was as fresh and alive as it was that day long ago it had set her afire for life.

Betrayed by an envious daughter-in-law ("Let's see her make those damned *belli, belli gnocchi mias* now"), she sat silently in the bus. Full of the old pride, she lowered her blouse and showed the mark.

The woman sitting opposite her was not impressed. She kept looking out the window for Jesus; she had felt it in her bones that this was the day. It was not fair to have to leave just when he was coming. She had fought hard when they took her, tripping the guard and trying to get the back tackle on him. He had snatched her sign —*Yes, He Has a Round Trip Ticket*—but she had held onto the flag. Old Glory. And now she hoisted it high in the bus. It was not legal without the flag.

Outside, people watched them go, waving and sorry

now, because they knew they would miss the funny, ridiculous things the old ladies said and did. There were no protests as there had been when the occupants of the nursing homes were stacked on the last trains and shipped out. "My God," people had said then, "the old ladies will be derailed. These trains are rejects from the New Haven." The buses were the latest models, with rest rooms and food machines and pill dispensers, much nicer, the onlookers agreed, than most of the old ladies were used to. The fact was, the old ladies were lucky; they wished *they* were going on such a nice trip, getting away from a stuffy, hot city. For the first time now many of the onlookers noticed the wall which they had previously thought was only a new housing development.

The buses rolled on through the gateway of the wall. When one bus sputtered and almost stalled, a few people ran alongside it, staying awhile with the old ladies, keeping them company on the journey, for some had begun to cry. Only one person tried to stop the buses. Though powerfully built and of athletic bearing, he was pushed aside. The bus bumbled on and no one else tried to halt the procession. An old dog, who had thought to the very last that he would be taken, broke from the guard and ran from one bus to the other searching for his mistress and scratching frantically at the doors. Slipping, falling, his eyes sick and wild, the old dog was then pronounced mad, a menace, and shot. And weeping a little for the old women and the dog, the people went back home.

The Leader locked the gate of the wall and slowly followed the people back into the city. He had stood close to each bus as it passed him; he had looked into the face of each old woman.

She had tricked him again. She was on none of the buses.

CHAPTER FIVE

"Special," said the sign on the buses. For many of the riders this was true. It was the first time they had boarded a bus without waiting for it, or for a seat, and this, added to the fact of their banishment, kept them in a mild state of shock. But under the leadership of a few, right as ever, they rallied and commandeered the buses. "Help, help," said the drivers, laughing, and headed back to the city where, enjoying the show, they waited in the buses, eating free candy bars they knew how to prize out of the machines. Bets were made: my busful of old ladies can break down the wall of the city quicker than your busful of old ladies. "Get 'em, Mom," they called out in encouragement.

Inside the city the usual percentage of air raid sirens blew and the Committee and the people took cover, or watched the bombardment from the tall buildings. For two days and two nights the old ladies battered at the glass walls of the city with canes and crutches and umbrella handles they had saved from the garbage cans. Using suet bags as slingshots, they stepped back and, whirling the bags for momentum, hurled rocks and stones at the wall; they had seen this done in biblical films.

Intrepid reporters came to watch the sight and some citizens tried to give belated aid to the old ladies. One newsman turned his microphone to a man digging a trench under the wall. Yeah, he was unemployed, said the man, answering questions. Yeah, a waiter. Did time hang heavy on his hands? Was that the reason he had rushed out so bravely, the only one to do so, to try to stop the buses? Nah, time didn't never hang heavy on his hands, said the man; he had a hobby; everybody should have a hobby for their health; you ever seen a person with a hobby get sick, have time hang heavy? Nah. The reason he had rushed out to stop the buses was it just hadn't seemed fair to him. Everybody against the old ladies and nobody to help 'em fight back. He believed in playing the game fair, like in his hobby.

What was his hobby? asked the reporter.

Catching people falling out of windows was his hobby, said the man.

Could he tell the listening audience how he got started in this hobby?

How he got started was accidental. Walking home from the restaurant one day, thinking about that dirty, lousy kitchen, he looked up and this person was falling. Instinctive, like in the gym waiting for a ball, he opened his arms and there it was. His first catch. A little child. Jeez, it did something to you, that first catch. None of the other catches could ever come up to that first one. He thought about it a lot, but it wasn't something you could talk about. Some things was too big to talk about. Correct, bud?

Who were some of the famous people he had later caught?

Well, they weren't famous till he caught 'em, explained the man. *He* was the one that made 'em famous. Only last week, patrolling the streets, looking up, he had caught a baby falling from the third floor. Right away they had put the kid on TV, had his own program now, one of them Cry Shows. Little kid like that getting this start early in life. That was the American way. Himself, yeah, he'd had several job offers himself, a couple from baseball teams, but he had turned 'em all down. They might interfere with his hobby. Anyway, his wife was working steady.

What was the next question? he asked the reporter; the old ladies were making such a racket at the wall he couldn't hear the question. "Pipe down out there," he yelled through the wall (often in the kitchen the clatter of the dishes had driven him nuts; one reason he had got this hobby). Did he have some pointers, asked the reporter louder, for the young people who might also aspire to his hobby? School had dismissed for the kids to make field trips to watch the buses leave; a theme assignment: The Day the Old Ladies Left Town. Could he tell these young people of his ambition, some unfulfilled wish?

Yeah, said the man, he had a message for the youth— to let 'em know there were still people with the dream.

That, no matter how tough things got, you could still have the unfulfilled wish, something bigger than yourself. That was his message to the youth. Lay off the drugs, kids. Get yourself a unfulfilled dream. Be like him. Are you listening now? Put the microphone further this way, buddy—his unfulfilled wish was to push somebody out a window and run outside and catch 'em on the way down.

Had he succeeded yet in his ambition?

Not yet, he was sorry to say, he had only near catches so far. But he thought he could do it with an old lady. They fell slow and sometimes their clothes—ever seen the clothes old ladies wear? everything they own sometimes —sometimes their clothes snagged for a second on a spike or a potted plant, giving him that little extra time he needed. What worried him though—was it fair? Should he count it when they got caught this way? Was it a good example for the young folks of America? He had rather do it straight, he didn't want to claim nothing he hadn't done fairly. Yeah, he had did a little track in high school, run the four-forty pretty good. Yeah, he was strong. Oh, about one-eighty. Five foot ten. Still worked out at the gym. That's what the kids today should do. Kick the drug and get the gym habit. Meet the right kind of people, kids.

The way he figured his ambition, he could get a job as a window washer (ever see an old lady with a clean window?), leave the front door open, push, rush down the steps, quicker than the elevator usually, and catch her just before she hit the pavement. No, babies were too squshy, hard to get hold of. He'd advise the youth of America to stick with old ladies. They didn't cry too loud, just that one little pulled-in sob.

Would he demonstrate for the listening audience?

Well, he wasn't no impersonator like some of them show-offs he'd heard on radio, said the man. Remember the fellow that did all the sound effects with his mouth? After he'd heard him he'd gone around for hours trying to go like a 747—whr-r-r—till his wife had stopped him. It was a trick, she said. The guy probably had a whistle concealed in his throat or had one of them cancer operations. A cheater. But sure, he'd try to imitate a old lady. Get the microphone closer. It went like this—Uh—uuh. Kind of low soprano, though some old ladies had a high alto, too. Sure, he liked music. His kid played the piano. When he came home from a challenging day at work on his hobby he liked his kid to sit down and play for him. Yeah, He liked Bach.

But did he really like *old ladies?*

"How come you ask?" said the man, astonished. Wasn't he trying to help 'em get back in the city? In fact, his grandmother had been an old lady. Yeah, she had fell. Sure, he liked old ladies. Walk down the street, see 'em sunning on the standpipes or the boxes in front of the supermarket, covering up the special sales signs, made you feel good. Shaking their legs a little, or holding their hands, high-veined, tight on the canes, they made you

think, God bless the little old ladies of America. He often
stopped and spoke to 'em. How you, Mom? Where you
live, Mom? Can I help you home and up the stairs or
something, Mom? Hell, he'd taken this special course in
window washing to improve his hobby and help old ladies. Ever time now before he shoved he washed a window. Sure, he liked old ladies.

"Shut up out there," he called now to the old ladies
beyond the wall. "I'm talking to the youth of America.
Don't just sit down and be no catcher, kids. Be a pusher,
too. Take the next step up the ladder of success."

The fighting at the wall went on. One old lady adjusted
her thick glasses, turned on her toes, pivot-wise, and, holding the flag high in one hand, let go the suet bag in the
other. All waited for the crash. The glass wall held. Con-
ferring, the warriors bunched and ran against the gate.
But the gate was firmly locked and the attackers, without
a key, fell back. And now a gas, irritating but non-poison-
ous, was sprayed on the old women who, beaten back and
exhausted, returned to the buses where the drivers wel-
comed them according to their showing at the wall, and
drove on.

As the buses passed through towns people would line
the main streets and call out, "Where's the circus?" But
if the old ladies tried to enter a town, an official blocked
the doorway of the bus and said, "Good God, no," and the
drivers started the buses up again. Some of the old ladies

now pulled small animals they had been able to escape with, and the gas had not killed, out of their clothing. Parakeets began to fuss, a tiny alligator crawled up the aisle. A cricket chirped and an old lady smiled.

Calmly, just like any other old time, she had opened her door one morning to put out her garbage—a cottage cheese container, a banana peel—and there it had been— a live cricket! Her natural assumption was that it was a roach from the Cy Weisenberg Collection next door, or a flea from the fairies' cat down the hall. Then she had seen it was different. It was like the day she had found the seed—a flying seed from a dandelion. She had just reached up and caught it as it floated through her room, free and easy as could be, a flying seed. Something about it had pepped her up all day; it told her to get on out there and buck it. If a flying seed can make it from heaven knows how far away, you can. That should have taught her a lesson about being a cynic so quick about things. Before, she'd been all alone, with no one even to help her smile. Then the flying seed had come, now this cricket.

As the bus jerked on she opened her pocket and looked in. Did you come from some nice place to bring me good luck, cricket?

And wondering what would come next, the old ladies settled down to their new life on the buses.

CHAPTER SIX

For a while after the old ladies left, commerce boomed in the city. New businesses appeared, new products. Concrete Protectors, handy appliances for hardy lovers who smooched in the cement parks, were manufactured—rip-proof, adjustable to fit all sizes, and pressure-sensitive backed. Hard hats, with the flag already embossed, were snapped up by the increasing number of concrete workers. Plastic trees, pre-gummed to stick to the cement, came in every known North American variety. Nose-stoppers to ward off the smell of the burning books were sold by licensed little men on street corners. Bookettes, empty cardboard forms that people could hold up like real books, kept the publishers busy inventing new formats. Revised editions came out each week, with high rag content. Jackets, free of ornament and print, made best sellers. Newsettes, blank sheets of paper to hold on the subway so the passengers would not have to look at one another, were delivered each morning in time for the early rush.

Everybody was young and prosperous. And bored. The silence was ominous.

Then the first great fires started and the people, eager for entertainment, gathered on the street to watch. A spirited band played "Hail to the Leader," the only tune allowed since the banning of music and the theater. The firemen did their firemen's leap from the trucks and attached the big hose. They opened the sluice and waited. An hour later, puzzled, berated, they were interviewed over the smoldering ruins. "We advanced with the ladder pipe to extinguish the blaze and the water refused to flow." Had they, the firemen, perhaps been negligent? Indignantly: "We approach a fire regardless of who originates it." The pipes were faulty, that was the reason the whole block of buildings had burned, they said, and while the smoke was still rising a siren rang in the next block. The band played "There We Go Again," illegal, and the people hurried to the scene, their holiday mood somewhat dimmed by the prospect of the damage and loss.

Is there a little old lady incendiary in town? they asked, for threatening leaflets had been received. "Down with cartoons of live turkeys before Thanksgiving, making fun of the turkey," said one. "Unsanitary, my foot," said another, addressed to the Committee. "They do it in Britain. Have a public box where everybody can go and try on the teeth that fit them." These notes were signed with tracks, like a pigeon or an old lady might make, unfamiliar with the pen. It was as if someone accustomed to a larger canvas, a wider palette of colors, had been forced to confine her talents to the leaflet form. Sometimes a wispy, golden feather would be stuck to the notes.

The hunt began for any old ladies who might have survived the banishment. Old ladies, as well as pigeons, were known to stay around the buildings where they had lived, or in the same area, and now many, missed in the first roundup, were captured by checking the registration list. The library and the art museum, second homes for the lonely, were searched; the day the Committee ordered the doors closed forever a few old ladies had hidden in the costume section of the museum and what they had thought a very safe place, the Government Documents Room of the library. But they were now brought out and banished. Thank God, this is the last, said the Committee members. We'll have some peace from fire and can get on with building our wall higher. Also combat property loss, now colossal.

Then the siren rang again.

The Committee members took a tour of the ruins, preferably those near a delicatessen. People still followed them on the street, trying to shake hands as the pictures were snapped, and the politician said graciously, "Hi, Harry," "How you, Joe," while the Negro watched suspiciously for a trick, a slight. "This is not lox," he said. "You got like the others," said the delicatessen owner. "Scorched haddock. Jewish soul food."

The Leader examined the standpipes. "Something is wrong with the valves," he said. "Rip out these Invincible pipes and order another brand."

"Unbeatable," suggested the politician at once.

"By God, this is a slur on my integrity," wrote the

president of the Invincible Company, but over his loud protest the old pipes were ripped out and sold as scrap. A new company bought them. For a week or two the city was without standpipes, a fact unnoticed since the old ones had not worked. Sometimes, though, upstairs in the office of the Invincible Company, the president would say, "Listen, do you hear a noise downstairs in the basement?" "Of course I do," said the vice-president. (How did this knothead ever get to be president and he just the vice?) "They're painting the old standpipes for Unbeatable, our new subsidiary." "Oh yes," said the president. "Make up a report and have it on my desk by noon." "It is noon, goddam it," said the vice-president. Everywhere he had worked knotheads had been president and he just the vice. It burned him up.

But when the Unbeatables were installed and did not work either, the Committee had a meeting with a management consultant, a graduate of M.I.T. For a fee of $10,000 he wrote a nine-page analysis and concluded: "They miss the old ladies. A certain current, running through the old ladies' bodies, flushes the fuse, warms the washers, and insulates the casings. This current is now missing."

"How about the plain fire plugs, unsuitable in shape, too low, too high, or sloping in design—the ones the old ladies cannot sit on?" demanded the Leader. At nights now he had a recurring nightmare in which the old woman would be laughing and he would be tugging at the desk again. "After all," he said, "certain positions are unattainable even by an old lady." He looked away, knowing it well: all over the world old ladies at that very moment were busy reaching unattainable positions. "Old ladies with sloping behinds are not allowed in this city," he said shrilly. "Why aren't these pipes working? Why don't these pipes produce the water?"

"Sympathy," said the consultant.

"Put the old men on 'em," ordered the Leader.

Now for a time it was a sight to see, dapper old gentlemen who hadn't done a real turd in years, aiding the city and bowing to passers-by, making the most of the limelight they intuitively knew would be brief. Bald as a bird's ass, eyebrows like surgeon's sutures, most sat quietly on the pipes, impressed with the dignity of the job and glad at last again to be useful. (Sometimes in the little rooms, idle, miserable, outshone, taunted by the old ladies, they had thought their useful days were over.) But several, taking a leaf from the more spectacular of the old ladies, performed in some slight way. One, gathering an audience, raced his wheel chair around and around, whirring and backing the machine as though it were a dancing horse. Another fell to the sidewalk, writhing in a contorted heap. For a time it looked as if this old man would make good. But those licensed to judge fits said, "It is not a genuine, spontaneous spasm. The grunts and the muscular jerks are not synchronized." Still twitching, the old man was disqualified. Yet, it had been a good show and Old Men Watchers sprang up over the city, and there was a festive air again, with the old men sitting on the pipes and the people strolling the sidewalks as in the pre, old lady days.

The wiser of the old men knew it would not last and waited cautiously, wondering if the old women were back of it, if they were for them or against them. When the next fire broke out they hopped off the pipes, cracking jokes about the hot seat. The fire engines appeared and the people watched the great hose attached. The band was silent; the plug was turned. The firemen advanced again and again with the ladder hose; they approached to extinguish the flames, and not a sprinkler worked. Saul's Stationery Store, Loretta's Lingerie, Sid's Deli, and Steinberg's Antiques Plus burned to ashes. The Committee made another tour of inspection. "How you, Harry. Hi, Joe." The lox, plain cod now, was passed. "Is this a real bagel?" asked the Negro. From all the talk, bagel, bagel, bagel, he had thought it would taste better. "Everybody got a equal bagel," said the delicatessen proprietor.

The pipes, after inspection, were ripped out and in spite of threats of lawsuit by the Unbeatable Company the contract was given back to Invincible, who consented, out of pure civic concern, as a public service, and at considerable loss, to take the Unbeatable pipes as scrap. Double time was paid at Invincible, which was good for the economy, suffering from the great fire losses, and in a few days new pipes were installed. Stung by the ingratitude, but pliable still, the old men were plunked back on them again. When the pipes did not work the consultant made another report. "It is not the same as the old ladies. The current is different. You simply cannot take the current of old men and expect it to be the same as that of old ladies."

Sent back into obscurity, the old men were apologetic and chagrined, though a few, rather huffy, had to have tranquilizer shots to quiet them. These old men were dying and they went around making as much noise as possible, dropping this, throwing that, as though to make their last movements on earth heard, as though to prove that as long as they were heard they were alive. They would wait to get home before they crumbled.

The Committee met with the consultant. "Tell me," said the Negro member, "is there a master standpipe, such as a master switch in electricity, where we could put *one* old lady and affect the pipes all over town?"

This was the first question he had asked; before he had just listened; he had seemed to want only to learn. The consultant was impressed. "Yes, one old lady might do it," he said. The Negro sat back, smiling but not too much, and the Leader gave out the order: "Find one old lady for the standpipe. We know there is one in town somewhere." Specks of grass had begun to appear in little pots all over town. Ripped out and destroyed, they were mysteriously replaced, and Old Lady Hunts were organized, with bloodhounds and cattle prods, as they had been in the old days.

A prize, a free visit for two at a fine hotel in Las Vegas, was offered for any live old lady. Men looked at their middle-aged wives speculatively but before their husbands could turn them in and get the reward for themselves and their secretaries, the wives would rush to the beauty parlor and get a new dye or facial. Some said the Beauty Parlor Syndicate, the only one prospering, had put up the prize; others that the delicatessen, sick of handing out free lox, had. The standpipe people had openly fought the prize, though they now secretly owned the beauty parlor business. Citizens, caught between, feeling the pinch, began to grumble quietly, then to complain. What about the air pollution? they said. What about the smoke from the fires? What about our economics? There is no longer a booming business in Concrete Protectors because the fires are burning the plastic trees and lovers no longer smooch in the park. Lovers have been run indoors; with nothing to do but make love they have started reading. Indoor lovers are making their own bookettes and newsettes. They are putting words in them. What about that? they said.

Some had been against the banishment, anyway; they needed the extra dollars the old people's Social Security brought in. Also it had come to light that some old ladies had had rather large bank accounts, money inherited in time for the nursing home and now too late even for that, and had taken their bankbooks or pure cash with them, concealed in the sweaters and shopping bags. Others had failed to reveal the complex workings of the household machines to the younger women, several of whom had been strangled extracting clothes from the washers; one had accidentally locked herself in the dryer for two days without her cigarettes. In isolated instances children had begun to cry for the old ladies and would not hush even after a good bop.

"Some Leader," said the people, out loud now, and they began to call him Lox, the Leader. "He cannot even catch the old lady," they said. Another note, signed with pigeon tracks, had been received. "No more zoos. Except for the animals who want them," it said. "If you want to see something in a cage, get in one yourself." The Leader, flipping the golden feather off the note, had the feeling that he was already in a cage, being watched, not with admiration, as a Leader should be, but with grim humor; he caught a secret smile on the Negro's face. And he had dummies, models from the department stores which hadn't yet burned down, put on the standpipes and the consultant from M.I.T. said, "God, have you *no* true understanding of the situation?"

The dummies were a failure; lonesome people stole them to take home. Pushed, nervous, running out of things to ban, the Leader tried frantically to find an old lady and almost wished he'd had a mother, for now the biggest fire of all burned down Wide Road.

"Get us an old lady damn quick," said the people. "Go after the buses, you."

"The buses have gone to Los Angeles," said a citizen who had received a card from his aunt; she couldn't keep from writing him no matter how cross he had been. "Greetings from L.A.," she wrote, forgiving to the last. He missed her terribly. "Come on home, Auntie," he wanted to tell her. "You can nest the sick baby birds in my shirt drawer if you want to. I'm fond of those stylish little specks on them now. Auntie, I don't mind if you use my golf clubs for walking sticks. That limber way they get improves my slice." But no further news or mail was allowed in or out of the city and that card from L.A. was the last news from the outside world.

"If the buses are all in L.A., then find other old ladies," ordered the people."

"Yeah, why don't you get some old ladies back in town?" the catcher of people, interviewed again, asked indignantly. Out of training, he was afraid his technique would get rusty. It was like a musical instrument, like Bach, you had to practice every day. Yeah, call him a sucker, maybe, but he took pride in his work. He liked things clean, the reason he quit the restaurant. Lousy, dirty kitchen where they blew on the glasses and spit on the skillet to see if it was hot enough. You get a steak done just right in most restaurants, somebody's busy in the kitchen spitting on the skillet. At the window-washing school he had been the cleanest one in the class. Some of the fellows would get up there and rub, puff, blow, and quit, like they had no respect for themselves or their work. "You should go wash your filthy hands," he had told them, "you're a disgrace to the trade." Didn't take care of their sponges and brushes, either. But him, he worked at a pane from all angles till he got it shining.

But who would be there to see the clean window after he shoved? asked the reporter.

Funny, said the man, the wife had asked the same thing.

Who *would* see it—the cats, the creeps, the distant nephews and nieces who, calling it a sad job, came to claim the old lady's belongings, emptying out the shopping bags, backing away from the roaches and the dirt, but poking behind the piles of paper, sure the old lady had left something besides the cat food and empty cans and used envelopes she could not bear to throw away? The creeps saying, "Oh," now and then, and "Poor Aunt Lucy, hon, it just makes me sick." "Yeah, we need a drink, hon." "What have you ever done for her?" he wanted to shout at them. "Leave the old lady lay in peace." Excuse him, youth of America, for getting worked up and yelling like that, but them creeps brought out the worst in him.

So who *would* see the clean windows and appreciate them? said the reporter.

He would, said the man. That was the important thing. If you can't respect yourself, how you expect others to?

67

"So when you gonna get some old ladies back in town so an expert can work?" he asked the Committee impatiently. "Quit breaking all the windowpanes in town with these fires and get the standpipes to working."

"A sympathetic hydraulic node," wrote the consultant in a new report, "to wit, the old ladies, transversing the elliptical hypernode, is missing. That's the reason the standpipes do not work."

"Then the person who can produce an old lady will be our great Leader, will he not?" said the Negro member of the Committee, beginning to talk like a Leader, putting the "not" way down at the end of the sentence.

"That's correct," said the people disapprovingly. Big black thing talking that fancy way, and that fuzzy hair all over the place.

In his office at the Invincible Standpipe Company the president patted the knot on his head and listened. It didn't sound like painting down there to him; it sounded a hell of a lot like pecking. He called in the vice-president. "Make a report by six o'clock," he said. "And have it on my desk."

"It is six o'clock," said the vice-president. One damn knothead after another, he thought, staring at the other's head.

My God, thought the president, is it getting bigger?

He went to the doctor. "Nonsense," said the doctor. "Of course hammers don't keep falling out of windows onto your head. Brush off that feather, though, and leave thirty bucks as you go out. Next."

CHAPTER SEVEN

She answered the arranged signal and he slipped into the hidden, darkened room. "Anybody see me come in, Mom?"

"Who else you think there is in this dark hole but me? Set down, Warren," said Elizabeth, "while I finish this beer."

"Can't sit now, Mom. We're through with the sit-in sociologically and psychologically. The time has come now to fuzz out your hair and *move* in."

"Leave the ins out, forget the sociological and the psychological, and set," she ordered. Gingerly, he sat on the edge of the chair and she told him: "Listen, son, and get a few things straight. I've scrubbed and washed, given and taken lip so you could go to college. I've cried, prayed, and cursed for you. Dressed neat, I've stood in them demonstrations in the old days with my mouth shouting, 'Now, now,' and my poor feet screaming, 'No, no!' So far I've done everything you asked me so you could get ahead on the Committee. I integrated like hell, then I had to separate like hell. I've spread myself out all over town so it would look like old ladies were getting in the way. I've acted like a nut and been a spectacle to see. Want to see me be a spectacle, Warren?"

"No, thank you, Mom," he said hastily. "I get the idea."

"I've even pretended I liked them stinking pigeons messing up the place. I've tripped the Leader with my cane and hid in this little room under the bed when they came knock, knocking, yelling, 'All old ladies out. Old ladies are taking up valuable space the young folks need. Banish all old ladies.' I've laid still in a cramp for hours after they've gone, scared they might come back and find me. All for you, Mr. Committee Man. I ain't saying I regret it, or that I don't question some of it, but I am *not* fuzzing out my good slick hair like a Hulu for freedom now or ever. Besides, I done bought all them wigs."

"The Hulu hails from Hawaii, Mom. Quite an interesting dance they got there, kind of a Missionary Twist, from the old New England element. Sort of a Puritan Patty Foot. Whereas our folks are the Zulu, a tribe of Southeast Africa, noted for their cruel, cunning, and mighty warriors."

"Hulu, Zulu, what's the difference? Next thing you be wanting me to take a Arab name."

"Ain't you got no race pride, Mama?"

"I got as much as you and had it longer," she said. "But I ain't fuzzing out my hair. What the hell has that got to do with race pride?"

"Look at it another way then, Mom. We want the Vaseline people to feel the pinch."

"Not me," she said. "I ain't got nothing against Vaseline. When I was a child we ate it. Government had this big poverty program. Save the Poor Folks from the Long Hot Summer, all that gab. We got all excited over it, gonna live like the others now, we thought, gonna be something, get some of the gravy. Gonna get a real little leather collar, with a silver tag on it, for our puppy dog. We'd seen it in Woolworth's when we walked up the aisles on Saturday, touching, when the clerks weren't looking, but not taking. My baby sister Tucky picked out a little knife and fork set for her doll, in case she ever got one. Well, you know the way that gravy trickled down to us? Three hundred gallons of Vaseline. With a note: 'Keep up your slick appearance and pray for food.' Some crook politician in the distributing office had stole the money and the food and substituted the whole state's quota of Vaseline.

"I remember the day my poor papa came home with it. Had to hire the neighbor's truck, then pay him off in Vaseline. Talk about people on a hayride; there my papa was bumping along on them Vaseline cans. Sometimes that was the only grease we had. Didn't call it the medium- or the high-price spread, either. 'Cause we didn't have nothing to spread it on. We had a fish now and then from the Gulf but we was real poverty poor. I mean, we was deprived of everything but Vaseline. We was lucky. Folks down the road got three hundred cans of Del Monte pineapple juice. Them kids had pineappleitis all the time.

Every time you'd wrassle 'em they'd fall down and go squirt. But not us Vas kids. Besides having the slickest hair in the county we was the healthiest kids for miles. Got so we called supper Vas. 'After Vas, Mama,' I'd say, 'can I go and play with Jeanette and Forbes?' 'Not till you've wiped your mouth,' she'd answer. 'Don't show off eating Vas in front of them poor white kids.'"

"That's what I mean, Mom. We done supported the Vaseline people so long we now gonna make 'em hire more black folks so we have more money."

"No, sir, I ain't putting the squeeze on Vaseline," she said. "I owe it my good health. Some ladies go around saying, 'I got cancer, I got cancer, got this big pain in my stomach. Make out my will quick. Don't leave nothing to them stingy kinfolks, though, that fix the plates in the kitchen, then bring it out to you, a few grits and some Jello spread out like it's a real meal. Leave everything I got to the helpless little animals, help the little animals on earth, God knows they need it, and them hungry little children, not them mean shits that don't put nothing on the plate, maybe a canned weenie, or a little bite of catfish on a cracker.' Doctor say, 'Don't talk so loud, lady. They other people in this hospital besides you. Get in front of that fluoroscope and hush. Uh-huh, exactly what I thought from the windy way you talk. You are eaten up with gas, woman.'

"Not me, though," she said. "I'm free as the breeze. Ain't had gas to this day on account of coating my stomach with Vaseline as a child."

"You just happen to hit it lucky, Mom," he said. "Now if you'll just listen—"

"Also I ain't ever had no trouble on New Year's Eve whooping it up. 'Coat your stomach with grease,' they say. 'Stay till the last bottle's dry. Don't be no kill-joy, drain it to the last drop.' Some of 'em try to hide a bottle on you when it gets late, figure you won't notice it by then, and sure enough a few folks drop out, but I always counted the bottles when I first went in and always stuck it out to the last. Waddle home sometimes, but I made it. No, sir, I got a warm place in my heart for Vaseline."

"Okay, forget the Vas deal, Mom. But come on. Hear them fire engines outside? The standpipes where the old ladies used to sit and sun don't work. Firemen come and attach the big hose and nothing happens. Because the old ladies are missing. Everybody in town is hunting a old lady. I've seen as good hunts on Broadway for a old lady, Mom, as I ever saw in the piny woods for possums."

"So they need a old lady back, huh?" She opened another can of beer.

"Yeah, the person who can produce a genuine old lady will be the ruler of the city."

"Ruler of the city, hmmm. Have a beer, Warren."

"No, thank you, Mom. I got to keep my mind clear today."

"Warren, beer has cleared up more minds than college has. Not that I ever had the opportunity of college. Course I don't want you to think I'm uneducated, though.

I continued my education as they call it at night school. But it's hard to fill in the gap from the fourth grade to the graduate level, Warren. There's a whole world of education in between there that you never catch up on. I made some nice old lady friends at night school though. One was a little old screwed-up key maker. Gonna set the world just right with them keys. Wonder what she's doing these days? Heard anything about an old lady like that in your travels, Warren?"

"No, I imagine she's locked up tight somewhere and the keeper got the keys. Don't worry about that college deal, Mom. You scrubbed and sent me there and today I'm gonna make up to you for it."

"Yeah, we've come a long way together, son. Remember down home me and you resting on the back steps of the courthouse crunched up in a corner, not hurting a thing. And old Judge Earl come down and say, 'Move that black bundle, woman, so I won't stumble. Get that black bundle out of the way.'"

"Yeah, he was talking about *me*," said Warren. "On the *back* steps, too. That's what I never could get over. The next night me and a bunch of kids went down and peed black right on the spot. Sort of one of the first pee-ins."

"Yeah, then we come up here and lived in that apartment without no heat and we dressed in all our clothes and huddled around pots of steaming water to keep warm. You remember that, Warren?"

"I remember," he said.

"Remember how them rats, cold and hungry as we were, come out to watch. And we played that game from down home. First one see a white rat slap the fellow next to him on the back for good luck. Remember?"

"I ain't ever gonna forget it," he said. "Old Whitey Rat has come out now, Mama."

"We been through some hard times together, Warren. Hating times. When your daddy died he died hating me, you, and everything that had held him down. But mostly old Whitey. I ain't got that hate in my heart for white people. Use 'em, sure, but don't hate 'em. Some is just as nice as they can be—like me—and some is just as mean as shit—like you, Warren. And some is just plain pitiful. Of course, if it came to a shoot-out I expect I'd go with my own people. But I don't see it has to come to that. That don't mean I ain't gonna fight for anything I think is right, though, Warren. And what about you, son. Are you doing right being crooked as the rest of 'em? Is that good for us, son?"

"Look, Mama. Sometimes I ask myself the same thing. Is what I'm doing good for my people? Am I serving my people being crooked? And you know, Mama, it takes about ten seconds for me to decide: Hell, yes, my people are The People. And I serve The People."

"And now you gonna make me Queen of the Stand-pipes."

"It ain't no more than I ought to do, Mama. You been a good old mom."

They looked at each other, veiled, on guard, yet remembering, almost close. He moved first. "Now why do you not then hurry? I'll be back in half an hour for you. I think them other crooked sons of bitches are hiding out old ladies too."

"All right, son. I better pack my glad rags."

"Oh no, Mom, don't bother to bring none of them old-fashioned clothes."

"What you mean, old-fashioned? I wouldn't feel right without this nice dress with my white ruffle. Every Saturday when we was kids down home we used to put a clean white ruffle in the collar of our dress for Sunday. Had to read a chapter in the Bible, too. We rushed through it like we was catching a train. I still do it, can't get over the habit. 'What the hell are you reading so damn fast for, sister?' the preacher ask. 'Slow down. We got a whole hour to kill here. The choir ain't even come in yet.' Where's the Bible?" she asked. "I'll give you a sample of how I can whip it off, Warren."

"Not now, Mom. Anyway, you ain't supposed to have no Bible. We done burned them bitches. Later, when we have the inauguration, you can give the address. You know, like the only thing we have to fear is what some folks do for their country. All that bull. About the clothes—from now on you gonna buy all your clothes at Balenciago."

"He the one with the split-level navel?"

"Him too. And you gonna have a fur coat out of strictly head mink, Mom. Not only that. You know that little paper frill the fancy restaurants put on the end of pork chops? *Your* pork chops gonna have mink frills, Mama. Your chitlins gonna be stuffed with caviar."

"I ain't ruining my chitlins with no ink spots," she said.

"Any way you say, Mom, but come on. We haven't got any time to waste. The old ladies in the underground are busy. Keep writing them notes: 'We Shall Return,' 'Someday we will rise and take the city.' Some people think the old fuckers are setting all the fires."

"You know no nice old lady ain't gonna do that, son. Sure you won't have a beer?"

"Mama, how you getting all that beer in this hideout? I thought this place beerproof except what I bring you."

"Warren, you and the Committee done banished the hell out of old ladies but you don't know a damn thing about 'em, do you? When a old lady needs a beer she has it. If she wants a Bible, she's got it. You and that half-baked Committee ain't gonna take anything away from an able-bodied old lady she really wants. Now what about them jewels for the Queen's crown?"

"You gonna have pearls, diamonds, and rubies, Mom."

"How about my earrings with the gold loops? I been wearing these since I was a child. My papa found 'em in Pascagoula, Mississippi. He was just walking on the beach in the late evening, like he did sometimes, trying to forget the Vas, and to get back his pride. Just him and the gulls and the big old Gulf. That's when poor folks, no matter how low they been beat down that day, feel like they own something big, like the ocean. Also it's a good time to catch them little fish that burrows down in the sand. Papa dug his toes in deep, hoping to catch some and this little thing stuck to his toe, a gold earring. Digging in with both feet, fighting off the gulls, old Papa stayed there till he found the other one.

"I often wondered who these earrings belonged to—a rich merchant lost at sea? A little drownded child?"

"Like as not it's some broad there, Mom, getting screwed in the sand. The earrings got uncomfortable, she took 'em off, and the tide snatched 'em."

"Couldn't have been no broad there, Warren, 'cause the beach ain't wide enough. Anyway, Papa brought them earrings home so proud, only thing he'd ever been able to give me so fine, and Mama got out the needle. 'No, no, no,' I screamed. 'Stand still,' said Mama. 'Make Papa feel big,' and she pierced my ears with the needle and run a string through the holes. At school it become the duty of the music teacher to turn the strings each day so my ears wouldn't get inflamed. Turning the strings to music. What do they turn the strings in little girls' pierced ears to now, Warren?"

"I got news for you, Mom. They ain't no little girls any more and most of them has their own private needle, so forget the gold earrings. You gonna have earrings with the biggest rocks in town."

"Bigger than my colored rocks?" she asked. "When I

was a child my best and often only playthings, Warren, was the bright colored pieces of rocks and gravel my mama tore from the craws of butchered chickens that had roamed the creek banks and picked out the gay colored stones for their own. Sometimes I pitied those chickens, robbed of their jewels and their lives, and I would cry before I ate them. Mostly, though, I never gave 'em a thought, happy with the colored stones. Us kids would swap 'em with each other, cheating when we could. I was one of the best cheaters you ever saw when it come to them little stones. So I think I'll take my rocks," she said. "They ain't easy to get these days. I done ransacked every chicken in the supermarket and I ain't found a little colored rock yet. Found a bullet once that said *Peace,* and a razor blade, but no little rocks."

"Okay. Take your goddam rocks, then, Mama."

"How about perfume?" she asked.

"In the perfume department you gonna have Channel 5, 4, and 2, Mama."

"I hope it smells as good as my mama's sachet used to," she said. "Mama used to open the trunk and call, 'Children,' and we would chunk down our rocks—that's when I done some of my best cheating—and run to smell the sachet. She had it laid out on the tray of the trunk in a little sachet pack. Tea olive. Presiding, and smiling so proud, she only opened it once a week so it wouldn't wear out. 'Children, children,' she called. I'd give anything to hear that voice again, Warren. 'I'm gonna open the trunk,

children, Sachet Hour, sweeties.' 'Yes, Mama, we're here.'
That was a good hour, half sweet, half sad. 'Don't stand
back, Tucky,' Mama'd say to the baby. 'Step, up, hon,
with the rest of 'em. Take your baby sister's hand, Elizabeth, and help her.' So I'd take poor little trusting Tucky's
hand and steal her colored rocks. Tucky was kind of shy
and backward; couldn't tell which hand was which. In
the fall when we'd gather the chinquapins she'd have to
jiggle the nuts to tell which was her right hand and which
was her left. Didn't seem to interfere any with her business, though. She later became a tart in Boston, Mass."

"I think I met that little old lady, Mom. I remember
when I was in Harvard one that used to say, 'Pardon me
a moment while I jiggle my chinquapins.' Naturally I
thought she was referring to something else."

"She kept her nose high, too," said Elizabeth. "I saw
her last summer in the Museum of Fine Arts. Looked like
any other little old Boston lady on the down-grade, spending the day somehow. 'Come up closer, Tucky,' Mama
used to say. 'Keep your nose up, precious, so you won't
waste the sachet smell.'"

"To hell with that Sachet Hour crap, Mama. You gonna
have perfume to flush the toilet with."

"Where am I gonna live, Warren?"

"Live, woman? You are going to *dwell* in a penthouse
in the tallest building in town. So high the birds can't
make it."

"You mean a Queen can't get to see the wild geese go

by?" she asked. "'Come, children, the wild geese is flying over,'" Mama used to call, and we would run out and wave to the wild geese. That was one of our big entertainments. We thought they saw it. I would have sworn one old goose did, the way he ducked down, sort of flipped before he caught up with the rest. 'Look, Mama,' I'd say. 'A wild goose is waving just at me.' 'Wave back then, honey,' she'd say. 'Tell him you'll see him next year. Make him feel like somebody care about him.' I waved my head off at that old goose, letting him know I care about him. Sort of shook my hand this way, Warren. Look. Here's how I done it. Ain't that a nice little old goose wave?"

"Mama, waving at wild geese is strictly passé, especially with a beer can. You'll throw him off the air current."

"Knocking the roosters off the hens was another entertainment we had. We thought they were pecking 'em till one day a old hen went after Tucky. I think of that often, how things turn out—little Tucky up there in Boston jiggling her chinquapins, and that old hen, fighting mad, deprived of the rooster. Sisters under the skin. Who knocks the roosters off old hens these days, Warren?"

"Most likely they have to knock the roosters off the roosters these days, Mom. Anyway, that's gonna be your department in the new government. You gonna be Official Wild Goose Waver and the Head Rooster Knocker Off-er. You gonna be boss of the Chinquapin Jigglers and live in the Tower, Mom."

"Ain't that the place the Committee meets?"

"Yes, ma'am, and from now on it's your home."

"The Queen Leader," she said.

"Correction, Mama. Your title's gonna be Queen Mother of the Leader."

"Warren, you don't know enough about how the world runs to be the Leader. You've gotten to be a hot shot in the Committee, but I done asked you three big questions here: Which is the right way to wave at a goose? What tune do they turn the strings to? and Who knocks the roosters off the hens? You ain't had the answer to none."

"All right, Mom, in this order: the Black Panther Salute, the string quartets, Mozart, naturally, and Invincible. They got a little electric knocker they do it with like the one they knocked out old ladies with. And now, if I've passed the test, will you please get the hell ready while I go to the Tower. You got to watch these crooked sons of bitches every minute. They'll do anything to hold you back, Mom. Yesterday they stole the engine right out of my car. Last week they was monkeying with my differential. Knocked the torque converter plumb out of whack.

"That ain't worrying me, though, Mom, as much as that rock-stealing deal you done. That ain't gonna look so good when they write up the life of the Leader."

"I'll try to think of another angle, son." She closed the door behind him and waited. When she no longer heard his footsteps in the hall she went to the kitchen door and opened it. "He's gone," she announced. "I kept yapping the old granny act to give you time to make the fire bombs like we learned at night school. You write the note. This is one time when being women together is stronger than being black together—and I'll get the beer and the Bible and we'll join the underground."

CHAPTER EIGHT

"Around the walls you see the temporarily discarded standpipes. Sitting on them are members of our underground, guardians of our culture."

Acting as guide, Sarah gave the new arrivals a tour of the basement underground.

"The group over here takes care of the music and art we've rescued to return to the people when we take over the city. Over there are the books we saved. In this corner the ladies are making posters to put up when we take charge." An old worker held up a sign: NO TRANSISTOR RADIOS IN PUBLIC. "The next group are tending pots of flowers and grass. Every night one of us slips out and plants one wherever she can break through the cement. Over here's the TV we saved. Some were for saving it, others not. We compromised. We don't use the sound.

"Under this chassis, working on the new-model car she's perfecting, is Sister Mary Magdalena, formerly head of the Station Wagon Division of St. Agatha's Abbey. On the eve of banishment Sister Mary was able to partially impair one of the buses. Tell them about it, Sister."

"It was nothing," said Sister Mary. Crawling under the bus at night in her jumper suit, she had found the screw in a moment. She'd turned it just as she had learned that day in the summer of her novitiate when she and that good-looking Italian monk had been mysteriously stranded for three hours on that lonely hillside road, with just their rosaries and prayerbooks. Get away from the conservative General Motors syndrome, he had urged her. Get into the little foreign-car field. Learn the joy of disengaging the transmission. Experience the fulfillment of installing a new muffler. Explore the differential, he had said, and had proceeded to do so.

"The vehicular emission will never be the same," said Sister Mary Magdalena, and disappeared again under the car.

Sarah continued. "Violence has no part in our plan. We are not revolutionaries. Though the radical fringe among us calls for action—storm the Tower, assassinate the Leader, free the political prisoners—we will play a waiting game. That does not mean that we have taken an oath of non-violence. Pushed too far, we will push back, as we already have. It does not mean we will fold our hands and depend on prayer. Unanswered prayers have sent more old ladies to their graves than spoiled tuna fish. It merely means that we will bide our time. Let the enemy defeat itself. It has the city but we have the key. We are our own best weapons.

"Simply, our plan is this. Our sisters aboard the stalled bus will be notified in time to return for the capture of the city," she said. "Honey, one of the pigeons above us on the rafters here, will be our messenger. These pigeons are our helpers, the only birds we could save. Mr. Randall, our head pecker, has found a way to unscrew the standpipes so they won't work. Though a trained and competent worker whose peck, hit, and error rates have been recorded in obscure psychological monographs, Mr. Randall was refused employment in the Invincible factory upstairs. Now, by pecking at the different flashing lights which are a secret and intricate system of take-over tactics devised by and for old ladies, he's able to dislodge the central screw. None of these standpipes, no matter how many times repainted, resold, and renamed, will work. Like Sister Mary, Mr. Randall is one of our most skilled helpers. Show them, Randy."

The pigeon on the great screw in the middle of the room jabbed faster and faster at the flashing lights. Trying to get the attention of the golden-feathered Honey, he did a sideways courting dance, remembered from outside. Beak gleaming, he hit the red on the nose, dived for the green, got it, and, with a quick glance at the golden one on the rafters, overreached on the violet.

"Can't win them all, Randy," said Sarah, and, the newcomers made welcome, returned to her writing.

Here in the underground where the walls were hidden by the standpipes, she had been temporarily forced to abandon her history of the banishment. But the urge to serve others was so deepseated, so a part of her New England ethic, that, finding her days here unfilled, she had, rather than be idle, instituted a private advice column. "Dear Mr. Epstein," she wrote, picking out a name from the Public Notices in the newspaper. "Have just read where your wife Estelle has left your bed and board. I gather from the double negative ('not no longer responsible') that this excessive charging has made you a nervous wreck. I strongly advise you to start a cantaloupe farm. There is nothing like it for a confidence builder. When as a child I visited my uncle in the Old South I was allowed to exhibit my prize specimen in the window of the bank next to Personal Loans. Every summer the word went out: The little Adams girl's cantaloupes are getting bigger and bigger. Others were considered prettier than me, as I am built on a rather awkward, sloping angle as so many New England ladies are, from, as my southern cousins suggest, bending over backward to prove a regional superiority. But it did me a world of good, standing on the outside looking in and thinking: But none can grow a cantaloupe like mine.

"When you get settled on your farm send me a sample. A sandy soil is best."

From the roost above, a pigeon registered displeasure with the whole setup in the most effective way he knew and, scrubbing the letter, Sarah defaced some of the words. Should she write it over or not? Cantaloupe, antelope, what's the difference? she decided, no strong speller anyway. Composition had been her best subject, service her motto. She was hungry now, and to keep up her

strength to write more letters—*The control of life and
death that people have over animals is wrong*—ate one
of the lamb chops that often appeared magically at the
door just when the underground was running short of
food. "God put them there," said one lady. "He should
get a local butcher," said another. "These lamb chops are
tough and from New Jersey. It's stamped on the back."

Strengthened for her more important work, Sarah sat
down at the key machine. The move to the underground
had hardly hurt it at all—only a minor scratch under
the hone control—and she began to pedal softly.

Some of her contemporaries at night school had picked
out flower arrangement and basket weaving. Sarah had
questioned the practicality of their choices. How could
they arrange one daisy, which was about what most of
them could afford these days? Oh, we will shove it around
from vase to vase, they said, dreamers. We will create The
Little One Daisy Arrangement. What could they keep
in the basket? Something will turn up, they said. There
will always be something nice for the basket. Sarah,
bound to her duty-before-pleasure discipline, had, in prep-
aration for a new life, for service to her fellow man,
chosen the Greater Opportunity course—Key Making and
Administration.

The other students in her class had been eager, clean-
cut young boys, and, with three of them, Eddie, Arthur,
and Louie, she had formed some of the strongest friend-
ships of her later days. Indignant about the way she had

been treated by the Leader, they would discuss it during recess as they polished the new keys, or in seminar where everyone criticized each other's keys, some acrimoniously and with no feeling of sensitivity for the creativity of others. But not her boys.

"You mean," said Eddie, "he did not come up to you and say, 'Look, Gran, why have you shut me out like this? The world's got to change. The old have to make way for the new. It's just history, Gran'? You mean he didn't even say that?"

She shook her head. "Just kept pushing and pushing the desk." Beside the ten bags of birdseed she had put in eighty pounds of back issues of the New York Sunday *Times*. "He fell flat on his face."

Arthur couldn't get over it. "If he'd just had the decency to say, 'It's not my idea, it's just the way the system works, Gran. Lots of smart folks like you have to give up to ignorant, forward newcomers like me.'"

"At least," said Louie, "he could have said, 'If I had my way I'd want you to stay right on so I could benefit from your superior intelligence and experience.' That's what Arthur, Eddie, and myself would have said, Gran. Watch it on the middle interstice of your new key there, Gran. You got to point it a little more like this, up and outward."

"It's got to feel like fine grillwork, Gran," said Arthur.

"Her goddam key is no good," said another in the seminar. "It's a goddam old-lady key and will never open anything but old ladies."

"It's one of the best keys in the class," said her boys.
When she graduated, the boys had built her the machine. To Gran from Her Boys, read the card. Call us whenever you need us. You will always be our Gran. Often at night as she practiced ("Don't forget your homework, Gran") ruffians would yell from the court, "Turn off that damn machine," but she had kept on until her interstices had become like fine grillwork.

However, that the key had opened the basement door to the Invincible Standpipe Company so easily had been almost a miracle; one quick turn of the wrist had done it. It was just one of those things that could happen in a million chances, she imagined. Unless you had taken a wax imprint of the keyhole the way Eddie had showed her in school. "It's all in the forefinger, Gran. The forefinger's got to be at a ninety-degree angle, yet still supple, Gran." There was no one as quick with their fingers as Eddie. In one week he had made 32,768 different keys, the total number possible, without milling grooves. "Gran is our Gran," said Eddie and, delicately milling a groove on the side of the key, made it 32,769. "We never had a real Gran before, Gran."

The boys had taught her all she knew, and now she could back up to any keyhole in town and own it. The trick was to hold your hands behind you and jab in the wax while you appeared to be merely resting. Eddie had showed her the exact little thrust to make. Of course she had clogged up a lot of keyholes that way but her percentage was high; by just acting like a crazy old lady, as expected, she had got imprints from the entire Committee's offices.

Her biggest project yet was in progress now, and when there was a rap at the door she quickly pulled a curtain over the machine (*Use it in health—Eddie, Louie, Arthur*) and shooed the pigeons to a higher roost. The workers stopped still, the flashing lights dimmed, and Sarah tiptoed to the door. "Give the greeting," she whispered. "Transversed any good elliptical nodes lately?" a voice outside replied promptly, and the scout was admitted. Shucking off her disguise, that of an old man, Gaelic type, she made her report. "People out hunting the buses, anxious for an old lady. Wind blew my beard off; I barely made it back; they chased me down the block." She pulled off the wig. "Of course, if I'd wanted to I could have let 'em catch me. Be Queen of the city now, have my own little pad." The old ladies looked at her and laughed, not loud. Homesick, they crowded around her.

"How do people look?" they asked. "Do they still look like people?" "Yeah, as much as they ever did." The bourbon-colored eyes darkened to a deep, thoughtful rye, a really good brand, premium. "They looked scared." "Shall we come out of hiding then?" asked the others, and held a caucus. The pigeons fluttered, eager to go, and some old ladies, troublemakers, showed posters, Give the Pigeon the Vote, but this was denied them. In the end the decision was: Never give up. *Take* the city.

Sarah went back to her machine. The colored lights flashed and in the center of the room Mr. Randall pecked at the screw. Again he missed; watching, the old ladies nodded wisely. "Poor Randy," said one. Out in the world she had been that way, too, pecking away, missing all the good chances for something; she couldn't recall for what now. Just one empty peck after another.

"Yeah," said the scout, shouting to be heard above the noise of the machine. "They'd say, 'Give Mrs. Ryan the best in the house.'"

Sarah shut off the machine and removed her chef d'oeuvre. Polishing the still warm object, she announced, "For the city gate."

The others touched it, admiring the fine grillwork, feeling the honed perfection. "We'll send it to the stalled bus to the recruits," said one.

"No," said Sarah firmly. "We will keep the key. We will send them the *message*. Remember Paul Revere?"

And the others quickly saw the advantage of this. Some who had thought her just another frustrated old New England meddler, writing those silly notes—Duty, Honor—broad a-ing it, and running that damn key machine, jij, jij, jih, jih, jih when they wanted to sleep, looked at Sarah with a suspicion bordering on downright respect. "You doing all right," said Elizabeth, the black woman. "You act like one of The People."

Sarah wrote the message "Return," and the scout began to pull back on her disguise. The others stopped her. "You are tired and have earned a rest," they said. "Honey is our volunteer."

Sick to death of the old ladies and the other pigeons (that jackass pecking his head off when the lights flashed and doing that corny hippity-hop dance at her), Honey had not yet had a chance to try out her wings, strong and gorgeous, mended now from the blow when she'd struck at the Tower window and fallen. One way she held them, she could see the golden sheen in her feathers; often she watched it all day; this had made her neck sort of crooked but interesting-looking; she could see the reflection in the TV sometimes. Rising up, up, now, Honey, who could never forget that day she had almost made it to the top, headed for the penthouses. In the basement doorway the old ladies, sad somehow, stood and watched the shimmering curve of the flight.

When Honey did not return in a few days the ladies, in council, chose Mr. Randall to find the broken-down bus.

This baby can handle the job, all right, the report from the factory where he'd sought the job had said. If only—

If only he were human indeed, fumed Mr. Randall, sniffing the foul air above the Hudson River. He had done everything perfectly at the factory test, touching the tool with a confident grace and sealing the capsules with a twist of the bill—easily, almost cockily. But the inspector would shuffle the capsule around in his hands like it was too hot to handle and say, "Oh boy, oh boy." The workers, watching, had laughed a little, too high, then grown quiet and passed stricter union laws: No pigeons or sons of pigeons unless their grandfather had been a member or from the right part of the old country. The president and vice-president, afraid, had refused to hire him. All he had been looking forward to was a pension and a nice life. All he wanted was a chance like everybody else. A chance with Honey. "Stay, stay," he had urged her, maneuvering for a mount. "If you think you've got it hard, how about me?"

Peck green, discard red, peck blue, discard yellow. Pretend you don't know the difference in the goddam colored lights. Throw 'em off the track. It was enough to turn your stomach. Rising, he thrashed angrily at the air. This pulled the message on his leg down and for a moment he dropped dangerously before he could regain his balance. He had never before flown this far at all; in the old days he had only gone from the trees in the park to the feeding grounds on Broadway. It had surprised him when the old ladies chose him for the trip.

He had tried to get it across to them: But I'm not trained. And he had begun to pant, holding his beak open and breathing in a noisy fashion that had always annoyed him whenever the old ladies did it. Pitiless, now, they watched him. "The trip is easy," said Sister Maria. "A bus with that transmission can only have gone far enough to keep them out of our way, but not too far for them to come back when we need them. Twenty miles at the most."

Twenty miles, for God's sake. He had known then how much he had grown to love the basement; the key machine; the posters; the scenic old standpipes—one day Invincibles, the next Unbeatables. He had tried again. Feathers drooping, he had fallen sideways and twitched. The old ladies had grabbed him and bound the message to him.

"Dispense with the disabled bird act," they had said. "We've read the pigeon books. We know you're supposed to make the trip at least once. We know we should take you out a mile and let you come back, next time five miles, and so forth. But we're old. We don't have that much time to waste. Certainly not on pigeons. We know that anybody who can peck the right lights like you do can find the way."

"Just play like you're a wild goose when you get up there," said Elizabeth, the black woman. "Act like you're on your way. With people below waving at you, hoping you make it. I'll wave to you. If somebody don't shoot you down first."

"Use the sun as a compass and follow the Hudson River," said Sister Mary Magdalena. "Pick out a landmark, the George Washington Bridge, and turn left. Get in a magnetic field, take Highway No. 6 to the New Jersey Turnpike and stop at the first Howard Johnson's.

Be your own navigator. Or just follow the cars. Someone will always be going your way."

Holy hell, he had thought, a talking nun. Freeing himself from the old women's grasp he had made an angry jab at Sister Mary's ankle. And who will do the pecking here?

"Oh, there will always be a pecker," said Sister Maria, giving him a Christianly kick that jarred his tail feathers.

Him, the goddamnedest best pecker in town. Boiling at the memory, he fought the air; then a thought cooled and calmed him. Soon it would all be over; soon he would take over from the old ladies. "It's a cinch," he'd told Honey. "I've found a pecking way to cut the electricity in the whole city. It'll be ours. The nun is not the only one who can turn a screw. We'll have a pigeon control system that'll open every door in town. Stay with me, Honey. Forget the penthouse." And showing off for Honey, he had done the pendulum motion between pecks, then gone counterclockwise, dizzy.

Try not to think about her, Randy, he told himself now. (Backing off against the wall whenever he flushed his feathers the least bit; it was damned humiliating, and the way the old ladies laughed, disgusting.) Conserve your strength for the flight into the bounding blue, old boy. Hold your best ones for the George Washington Bridge.

Near the bridge he paused, confused by the long lines

of traffic. Turning right, he chose the wrong lane of cars and ended up at the Eighth Avenue Subway Station. Reversing, he headed west and crossed above the bridge to New Jersey. There a Volkswagen he had counted on— "Follow a little foreign car," said Sister Mary Magdalena —led him a wild goose chase on Highway 4 and he had to backtrack to reach the turnpike. The speed of the cars and trucks was frightening, and, looking down, he closed his eyes.

Then above him a giant jet zoomed by. Scared for a moment, he cowered—Jesus, what a bird!—then pushed on, head high. No matter how fancy they built it, with how many engines or jet holes, the airplane must still have the shape of a bird—a bird shaped like a shark, perhaps, but still a bird. That is the triumph of the bird. A bird is the ultimate.

Now he rode the wind high in the yonder, coasting, enjoying it, winning. Below him the houses and the highways were like toys. The tiny dots looked like people, real little humans.

Three hours out, his wings tensed; he sniffed the air: Howard Johnson's, the luncheon special. Then below him, off the ribbon of highway, he sighted the camp. Right about where Sister had said, he thought, with grudging admiration. From the air, with the bus seats in a circle, and a fire in the center, it resembled one of the TV westerns the old ladies, for laughs, watched a lot in the basement. (Honey would sit and watch it, too, but he would watch Honey.) Lowering his altitude, he came in, set for a perfect landing. Then suddenly, on the alert, he rose again. Too late, he ducked, knowing somehow now that the old ladies in the basement had guessed his plot and sent him to his death.

Using a suet slingshot, an old lady from the camp bagged him and ate him with her pearl-handled knife and fork.

CHAPTER NINE

As fast as the old ladies in the underground sent out the pigeons, those in the camp killed and ate them. Mixed with french fries from Howard Johnson's, they were a welcome change from the diet dispensed on the bus. When no more pigeons came the campers sat around the circle of seats from the bus and waited for the next thing to happen.

Even at the beginning, as it creaked out the city gate, it had been evident that this bus would never get far, and when at last, across the bridge, left behind by the other buses, it gave a warning sputter no one had been surprised. The driver jabbed at the gas and kicked the starter, but the old ladies, jarred almost into insensibility, were relieved when, with a final wheeze, the bus crept off the turnpike into the grass and died an almost human death. Hunting hidden treasure, the driver pulled the seats out, shook them, and arranged them on the ground as though he were doing a favor: Look, seats for Mother. The old ladies, using him, clever at this, let him sweat and hustle, very particular that he set the seats just so, out of the draft and near the shade. A few waved good-by when, ostensibly leaving to get help, he deserted.

A turnpike policeman came. "No stopping except for emergency," he said. "Speed up." The old ladies stared at him like idiots, a way they had learned was useful, and he went away to think about it.

The old women tried to live in the abandoned bus and slept stretched out on the floor or outside on the grass, gazing up at the stars. In the daytime they would hurry to the road and wait for the explanation: A mistake, Mama, just a joke to test your responses; something new we read for geriatrics. But the cars all whizzed on by and the old ladies quit this; some never went at all.

At night they huddled together around a campfire. As she had done all her life on the subway and bus, one attempted to assign seats with her cane, but there were cries of rebellion now and the old ladies butted heads, like antlered deer, and won their own spaces. Soon there was position and tenure as there had been on the benches and the standpipes. Sometimes around the campfire they sang. A chorus of "Belli Gnocchi" would follow one of the rousing work songs, "Sew, Sew, the Suet Bag Sew." Often there was the cry "Thief, thief" and the old ladies with money said others had stolen it, or it would not be money perhaps but something more precious, a sliver of soap or a fine-tooth comb, or a little wine they had saved, calling it paregoric. One lonesome old lady who for company slept with her hand on her bosom would wake, crying, "Who stole my titty? Where's my titty?"

Once she had had a great tit, much in demand, and the boys had come, imploring her, "Show us the tit, show us the tit." But she would not show it, and now it was gone. Why? Where? It would haunt her dreams always that she had not shown it before it was stolen—The Great Tit.

At night, real thieves, or teenagers, stole the tires and the gas from the bus, and finally the fenders while the campers, afraid, pretending sleep, watched them. Frequently one of the old ladies, muttering, or perfectly silent, wandered off from the camp and never reappeared. The others would look for her, but not much, and in a few days she would be forgotten. Others would move into her place by the fire. Some were killed crossing the turnpike, tying up traffic for miles, infuriating travelers headed for the shore. The police came back. "How many times I got to tell you to step up?" he said, and the old ladies would move faster for a while, then forget.

During the day they sat on the seats or wandered about the countryside near the bus. A hydrant that said Water for Your Pet was close to the exit and the campers could drink and bathe some there, or at Howard Johnson's. Some brought back discarded rolls from the restaurant or wildflowers they would hold all day until the flowers died. One, Marjorie Jo, took her flag to the turnpike and stood there, waiting for Jesus, who went on by, took Exit 19, then turned south. A truck loaded with chickens, however, screeched, slowed and overturned in front of her. The driver, new to the course, had taken one look at the flag, the face, the message on the sign—*Slow Up for the Jesus Break*—and flipped.

Coralling the chickens, shooing them into the bus, the more commercial of the campers, some who had worked in the shops on Broadway, had an idea. "Go back to the turnpike," they told Marge. "Act natural." And a kind of commune was formed. They raised chickens. They sold three hundred crates of slightly smashed strawberries. They got into the bruised tomato market. They were able to offer at discount sixteen color TVs and twelve hundred Little League catcher's masks.

But the merchants of the near town objected and the old ladies, victims of economic politics again, were deprived of their newly won independence and sank back on the bus seats, waiting for something else to happen.

Twice a week the Foundation sent a man to refill the food and pill machines in the bus, but could not help further for fear of losing its tax-free status. The Turnpike Commission came and mowed the grass around the old ladies, and from the town nearest the camp a church sent a mixed chorus in choir regalia to sing. Their naps interrupted, the campers dozed and snored on the bus seats. The choir was disappointed; they had thought the old ladies would appreciate it more. "That mournful stuff," said the few old ladies who were awake. "We want something peppy."

It became fashionable in the town to drive out "past the old ladies" for entertainment, as it had formerly been to drive to the town dump to see what else people were throwing away. Then some in the town began to complain. "They should be arrested. They're spoiling the landscape. Our ecology is shot to hell. They haven't improved the property a damn bit."

"It is inhumane to arrest them," said the mayor's wife. "Let them have their nice outdoor summer camp. Some have never been to camp before."

"Yeah," said the police, glad of an out. "Look, they even got a flag. It's legal."

"Listen, we went out there and sang our hearts out," said the choir, "and for what? Old ladies, empty capsules, and feathers all over the place. We call it an eyesore." But the mayor's wife, an aging, lilting girl, said, "Let's call it I Soar instead. Let's give the old ladies a lift." "Oh, Christ," said others, "there she goes again." Lift was good, they said. Why couldn't the mayor get it up more often so this dame could be satisfied at home? A few of them privately met with the mayor in an advisory capacity: "You are carrying too heavy a load. The job is too big for you. You need an assistant."

"We must teach these poor dears some arts and crafts," said the mayoress. "We must keep them out of mischief and interested in life. Even I feel the need sometimes of something higher to fall back on." "Try the Harvard Business School," said the mayor's advisers.

THE BANISHMENT

"We will send them a yoga teacher," said the mayor's
wife. "We will teach them to sit and meditate." Nothing
new to the old ladies who had been sitting and meditat-
ing for years, yoga was a failure; some thought she had
said yogurt and were pretty mad when none showed
up. But the mayoress did not give up. "We will buy
them a wheel and send them a potter," she said.

A dainty-fingered young man from the Y, with a portable kiln and real live coals, came, a sure enough little
potter, and, looking down at the old ladies circling the
bus seats, he talked of the craft, of coiling, of the wheel,
of a pot philosophy, of the true pot, how the true pot
was within yourself. He had been right cute, telling
about it, of the boundless joy, the limitless pride, the
immense feeling of fulfillment the *inside* of a pot, the
very hollowness of it, could give you. This tickled the
old ladies; pretty silly, they thought, and they went
along with it. A few, corny, acty, went around saying,
"Oh, God, the hollowness of it." "Sure," said others,
"why not?" Fill it up with sixty-seven flavors of Howard
Johnson ice cream and they'd have a sense of fulfillment
too. Used to variations on this one (at the Y the boys
were just awful sometimes), the potter laughed merrily
and said of course you had to have an *outside*, too, if
you had an inside.

The old ladies disputed this. How did he know? Some
of them had grown up with pots without any outside;
they'd gone to school with them. "Listen, in Texas once

112

there was this big empty pot—" "It ain't possible." Charmingly ungrammatical, he smiled, trying to amuse the old ladies, to win them over, but to take charge at the same time. Who had thought it would be so hard? But did he really care? they wondered. Was it all put on? They thought it was (Look at those sissy sandals) and lined up on the seats against him.

Some would not join in the pottery class at all. What did old ladies want with something dead like pots and vases? Old ladies wanted something alive like chickens. At the garbage dump they found a bench and after that they sat on the side of the turnpike, as on the Broadway benches. If anything alive went by, they would see it.

Quick to sense attitudes (you had to be quick at the Y), the potter tried harder. The inside was the thing that counted, he said, especially that little part away up under the handle, and the mouth that absolutely nobody, not even the Japanese, had found a way to see. How about the Greeks? asked an old lady. The Greeks had seen everything and named it, and made all those vases, too, rows and rows of them in the Metropolitan Museum. She had spent hours at the Met, killing time, waiting, going to the special exhibits, hunting the toilet; why did she always end up in the vases? Forty acres of art and she got the vases, everyone of them just alike. A person of Greek parentage, living in Japan, who had seen all those vases could do it, she bet.

No, absolutely not, said the potter with finality. "Well, I declare," said the other old ladies, impressed momentarily, and thinking now that he was gaining their favor, he relaxed, skipping over the camp seats in a ballet step he practiced sometimes in front of the mirror. "Oh, people may *think* they have seen it," he said, bringing his toes to a full stop. It had been tried many times in many ways, he said. A film had been dropped inside and a photograph made, and under water, too, but no matter how they had tilted it, that part around the opening had come out dark and mysterious, with fuzzy edges.

"It's full of roaches," said one old lady. "You should get the exterminator." But another in the class nodded wisely; she had seen the very same Japanese movie. What a bore. Not a soul in it like Gregory Peck or Natalie Wood, someone you could identify with.

But was not this like everything else in life? asked Mrs. Jameson, another old lady. You got out of the pot what you put inside it. If you couldn't see up at the top of the pot that meant you hadn't put anything up there. You had put it all down at the bottom, like all the Negroes and Puerto Ricans and Democrats trying to get something for nothing. Good, good, said the other old women, nodding approvingly, for though he was lovable, something about the young potter got their goat. Look at him loping around the circle of bus seats, relaxing like that, when he ought to be up there teaching them something interesting and uplifting. And now they wanted Mrs. Jameson to be their spokesman against him. Not actually mean, yet there was something in them that said, Make it as disagreeable as possible for him.

"The pot hasn't been made yet that I can't see the insides of," said Mrs. Jameson. "Or a potter, either." And the other old ladies said, "Tell him, Jamesy." The young man eyed her; usually old ladies *loved* him and brought him little presents. At the end of class they always clapped and sang "He's a Jolly Good Fellow." Why had these turned so against him? Hello there, welcome, dear, to class. He'd gone out of his way to greet each one in the circle personally. "Hello, sweetie, aren't you beautiful in your crepe-de-chine robe and your pretty white socks and high-heel shoes. Aren't you nice to dress that way just for me," he told one expectant old lady. "Brought a flag, too." And he looked behind him to see if there were somebody else she was expecting, possibly a visitor of higher rank, perhaps the mayor, for after one good look at him through her thick spectacles, the old lady ignored him and kept her eyes on the road.

He turned back to Mrs. Jameson. "If such a pot has not yet been made, why don't you make one, dear?"

"Why not?" said Mrs. Jameson. "I will make a pot and decorate it with an old lady in banishment making like yoga. We'll sell it to the Metropolitan Museum," she said firmly. She was used to having her own way. On the subway when she said, "Take that seat," or at the rooming house when she put up signs—*Remove those news-papers from the hall, Don't cook fish where I can smell it*—she was obeyed. But the other tenants had turned her in to the Committee the first chance they got. Challenged now, she threw the clay on the wheel and, working fast, centered it. Nothing was new to her even if she had never done it before. Kicking the wheel in a burst of speed, she twirled her hands gaily in the air as though plucking a harp, mocking the potter. The other ladies, wadding soft clay into wire-haired terriers or grounded birds, stood around and watched her. Pulling the clay upward, thinking how she had almost got a bull's-eye on the Leader's head that time—an inch more to the left of the ledge and she would have got him with her begonia —she made the shape just right, wide at the mouth but not too wide. Big enough, though, and the potter cut it off the wheel.

"Now it will have to dry." He fired the kiln and the old ladies went out and called people from the turnpike and from Howard Johnson's. "Come on over, see the side show." Mrs. Jameson was embarrassed. "It's nothing," she said. "I'm only going to prove for once and for all that I can look in the pot. Anybody with sense can do it." "Oh, don't be a kill-joy, Jamesy," said the others. "When will we ever have another pot-looker like you?"

They looked at her as if they were seeing more than they had seen before and some of them laughed away back of their eyes. Switching their allegiance, they were against her now.

When the pot was dry they loaded the kiln. "It'll take two days," said the potter, nerves jangling from the old ladies, for him one minute, against him the next. He went back to the Y, leaving the kiln, around which the old ladies sat at night and baked salty teacakes and told stories about other kilns. Many had sat around better. "Why, in Princeton once," said one, hitching at her underwear, "right before the game—" Then she shut up quick. (Who here among these blank-eyed ghouls could know the utter thrill of it? The sleepless nights of reckoning, and he in his football suit, all ready, but so awkward then, pad, pad, buckle, buckle, not the new easy fashion, zip, zip.) Oh well. She looked into the fire, counting the coals.

The third day the potter came back. "It is not yet ready," he said of the pot. "Oh, sure it is," said the old ladies, impatient. "Are you trying to tell us how to make pots?"

"It needs more firing," said the potter.

"Firing, schmiring, what's the difference? The crowd's already gathered. The show must go on. Get up there, Jamesy, stick your head in and tell us what you can see. Don't mind Junior here."

"O-*kay*," said the potter, "but it *does* have to cool," and he was firm about this.

117

When it was cool he put the pot in the middle of the circle of bus seats and stepped back. "Put your face in it, Jamesy," said the old ladies. "Put it away down there and tell us all about it." They moved in closer to see; perhaps she would smother. Bending over, breathing noisily into the pot as though she were taking a cold cure, she tried to see all the insides. For a few moments she saw nothing and felt only a relief not to be looking at the old ladies and the pleading look in the potter's eye. Why should she have to look after him? she thought. It was enough to look after herself out there in the middle of nowhere with these nuts, and besides, he should not have become one of what they called those old fairies; he should have just said no, as those in the rooming house did when they were too tired.

"It's just an empty pot," she reported.

"Look further, Jamesy," said the other ladies, and winked at one another. "What do you see now?"

She would have liked to be inspired by the pot, to have reported philosophically on its contents—a message from the English-Speaking Union or something from one of Ike's books. "Nothing is in the pot," she was forced to say. "Look where he said, up under the opening. Do what he said you couldn't do," urged the old women. And she looked again but the part up under the mouth escaped her, as the teacher had said it would, for who could see it? Who could twirl their eyes around on stems to see around the opening? The Japanese had tried it, of course, furnishing little mechanical eye twirlers with each pot, but they had not worked on non-slanted eyes and tourists who came home with them were mad as hops.

"Can you see under the opening?" asked the young potter coldly.

"No, but I can darn sure feel it." Miffed by her failure, she stuck her hand inside, feeling the limitless pride, and all the rest of it, plus a big rough blob where at the crucial moment of the molding, when excitement ran high, another nervous old lady, imagining seeing it in the Met, their *own* vase, had jogged the wheel.

By now it was plain that the pot had been taken from the fire too soon. It began to shrink, and Mrs. Jameson's hand, arthritic, had begun to swell until it caught on the blob and the old lady was unable to withdraw her hand. "Pull on it, Jamesy, pull hard," cried the old ladies, and tried to fluster her; perhaps she would pull her hand off. Getting his revenge now, the potter cried, "Do not smash the pot. Do not smash the pot." The old ladies, taking the other side, switching again, chanted, "Smash the pot, smash the pot." The potter stepped back, wondering what the hell he had meant, Do not smash the pot? How could it matter to him, for God's sake? The old ladies drew away. What had they meant, Smash the pot? Why had they said it?

And now, turning again, they cried, "Smash the potter. Smash the potter."

That had broken up the class, but Mrs. Jameson had

kept her pot intact, wearing it thereafter on her hand like a catcher's mitt, or pretending it was not there at all. Sometimes when the old ladies grew restless around the circle she had to hold it high to protect it, and sometimes she nested it in her lap, like a pet. Other times she didn't know what to do with it; she knew only that it came to mean a great deal to her, though it was hard to explain her attachment to it. It had completely ruined her crocheting the suet bags and any further arts and crafts study, it had changed her direction in life, but it had made her expert at hailing taxis, if there had been any to hail and if she were going anywhere beside the weekly ride on which her son from Connecticut still came faithfully to take her. Called on to give a quick hand signal, she often tied up traffic for miles. "My God, Mama, pull your hand in," said her son, and drove her back to camp.

Class over, the little potter later tried to retrieve his kiln, but the old ladies claimed it, and shaken, pursued— "Where's my titties? Make him give them back"—he fled back to the Y to recuperate. Now the old ladies began to make pot after pot, almost frantically, as if with something in mind, and when they could find the material or rip it from the bus, they added melted lead or metal. The mayoress, assisting the mayor's new assistant, sponsored no more uplift programs.

The curious still dropped by from Howard Johnson's, and the policeman came back. "That's right," he said.

"Speed up, speed up. Stay in the right lane." But whole days passed when the campers saw no one but the man from the Foundation who filled the pill and food machines, and the people who whizzed by on the turnpike.

Still there was something in the air besides the smell of gas and frying food. There was a feeling of impending crisis. The old ladies scanned the skies, as though looking for a winged messenger or Helicopter 710. And along with their leaded pots they began to store up morsels from Howard Johnson's. Marge went back to the turnpike. There were a few minor wrecks—a thousand gallons of marshmallow topping, a shipment of ball-point pens— but the old ladies were waiting for something else. When the old scout finally staggered into camp they were ready. "Twenty miles, my foot," said the scout. "It's a hell of a long ways out here. No wonder old Randy didn't make it." And she gave the message. "We can take the city now."

CHAPTER TEN

Some refused to go. They had got used to life on the turn-pike, to the ceaseless swish of the racing wheels. Caught up in the social whirl at Howard Johnson's they could spend all day on the outside looking in, or, watching their chance, slip in with a family as though they belonged somewhere. They might even use the rest rooms.

Some, remembering the success of the commune, set up a stand by the nearest exit sign and waited for accidents.

A few loners went their own way. One began to fix up camp for a new life. Never before had she been free to have patio furniture or a pet and now, any time she wished, she could search the garbage dump for a nice wrought-iron chair with no bottom or a homeless kitten. When somebody or something she loved died she was no longer shoved into the hall to cry. Nobody could say, "Hush, hush, don't cry so loud. Who wants to hear an old lady cry so loud in the hall?" She had her own home now. She could cry in privacy.

But most of the campers, homesick, armed themselves with a pot from the kiln and began a rag-tag march. What fate they were going back to they hardly knew or cared.

They missed the city. They were going home to the excitement, the danger, and the hit or miss of everyday life. Out here at Howard Johnson's even the parking was cut and dried, with lines marked to show you exactly where to go. The creative parker was prohibited. Except for a good spill now and then on the turnpike it was pure Dullsville.

Following the back road, away from the turnpike, they marched on, mostly at night. When they weren't too dizzy to look up they began to locate the stars and point them out; if they could not recall the correct ones they gave them names of their own—a town they were from, Albany, a flower they had liked, Freesia, a favorite restaurant, Schrafft's or Lum Fong's New Asia.

Living off berries and water and bread, sleeping in the daytime, footsore, weary, they marched on. Sometimes the scout slipped into a town as they passed on the outskirts and brought back news: the old men were trying to replace them in the city. This tickled them—when had old men ever had the guts of old women?—and now they laughed and marched on with a springier step. As they tramped the back alleys they sang softly, "Mine eyes have seen the glory," or a stirring Princeton football song.

Using the pedestrian lane, they crossed the George Washington Bridge at night. From the bridge they marched south and bivouacked on the banks of the Hudson. Rats from the waterfront came out to watch and the old ladies took turns at guard duty. The next morning

they marched toward center city. Entry to and exit from
the city had long been prohibited and the road was theirs.
There were laggers now and the front ranks, as they
waited for them to catch up, argued heatedly about questions they might soon face again.

Question: was it safer to take your money with you
when you went out, liable to muggers and purse snatch-
ers, or leave it at home for picklocks and robbers?

Decision: they had you either way.

Question: should you make out your flight insurance
to the person who drove you to the airport, even though
you wished to leave it to another?

Answers: (1) Yes, if no one else offered to drive you
and he looked over your shoulder while you filled out the
form. (2) No, it was probably the reason he offered. (3)
It depended on how bad the traffic had been.

"Nonsense," said Marjorie Jo, hoisting the flag. "Jesus
will pay the insurance when he comes. Jesus was our
first flyer to get the return rates."

Question: what should one put on the tombstone: *Did
We Win?* or just plain *We Won?* Do you *have* a tombstone when you're cremated?

No, but you have an urn which is only a storage. We
will make our own. We will put on them: They Hath
Earned Their Own Urns.

"Put *Jesus* on the pots. Put *Jesus Will Win.*"

Following the flag, the old women crept back to the
city.

CHAPTER ELEVEN

For some time there had been a feeling of disquiet in the city, though there was nothing you could put your finger on. Cars parked one place at night would show up in another, expertly dismantled. Parts would be taken and returned, slightly used. Often there would be a vague, disturbing sense of unseen presences, of swift passages in the night. Sometimes there was a noise as if someone was trying to break through the cement, and the next morning a flower or a pot of grass would be found growing. At other times a sound almost like real music could be heard and the people would hurry to the door and say, "Listen, listen." Then it would stop and, tired and dotty now, they said it was just the stone whistles, a sideline Invincible sold, that they had made up to sound like birds. A certain way the wind blew, they sounded like sick birds calling, some said.

At the office of the Invincible Standpipe Company the vice-president said, "We are repairing the Unconquerables, that's all. This sentimental shit about bird singing is ridiculous," he added, insulting the inventor of the stone whistles, who had tried to make them sound as much like a real bird as he could. It had not been easy working on it far into the night, with his wife yelling, "Come on to bed. What does it matter how the whistle sounds?"

"It matters," he said.

"Listen, it's stone, it's a whistle, it blows. So what you want? You want to blow an old lady out the end?"

"I want it to blow like a bird," he said.

"Look, hon." She sat up in the bed. "I been trying hard to do it right. It's just that I'm tired from doing all the work your old mother used to do before the Banishment. Boy, am I bushed, cooking, cleaning, washing all day. I'll try to do it better, though. See. Come on, hon, look now. I'm making like a whistle. Look at the birdie, hon."

"It's not that," he said.

She screamed: "Then why do you care so much about the damn bird whistle?"

"I care," he said. Going to bed that night, listening to the sick bird song, people thought, What is this feeling of unrest? Of creeping things, a muffled sound, as of marchers on old feet? Who is coming?

CHAPTER TWELVE

"Having rendered the sentries at the city gate ineffective, by a method which I am not yet free to reveal," Sarah would later report to her writing wall, "we occupied their posts and from these vantage points awaited the recruits. We could see them coming from a long ways off. At first, straggling in a thin line, they appeared to be figures from *Don Quixote* or ghosts from the Book of Revelations. Then the flag came into view and we of the underground force went forward to welcome them. They were tired from the long march and many of them, Daumier-like, stark-eye, dazed, rat-bitten, rested a moment against the wall.

"Then we opened the gate for them and they filed quietly into the city. Keys hot off the machine were distributed. Too nervous, some of the ladies passed out, but replacements came quickly forward. There were a few knockdowns at the gate, some of our new recruits, over-eager, assaulting members of our own ranks. We advanced to the center of the city. There was a slight skirmish, here again in error, where a few winos and prostitutes thought we had come to displace them. When the people awoke we had already marched to the government offices.

"Four of us, for obvious reasons, were chosen to go to the Tower. The Leader, coward, had already fled before we arrived; the others were surprised hastily packing their papers to escape. The politician tried to join us. 'Why, hello there, it's good to see you ladies,' he said. 'My goodness' sakes alive, if it's not my good friend Miss Emma.' But after one look at Miss Emma and the leaded pot, he left, and not until the next time will he try to fool little old ladies again. Mr. Mamamia was easy. Belli Belli had only to grandly bare her gnocchi; stunned, the poor fool genuflected and ran. The Negro was the last to go. 'The best goose-waving window's over there, Mom,' he said, then he left too.

"A favorite family joke, perhaps," wrote Sarah. "I detected a note of real affection in his voice. It is not inconceivable that at one time even the Committee members must have been human. I almost felt sorry for them when Sister Mary Magdalena, arriving in her new car, was able to turn a surreptitious switch and trap them in the ninety-first-floor elevator for several hours.

"Leaving the Tower in Sister Mary's car, we had occasion to pass through one of the busy sections of the city. Traffic stopped to let us pass. People lined the streets to cheer us on. We nodded, acknowledging the acclaim, and, though we felt slightly foolish, even allowed ourselves the extravagance of the victory salute. Miss Emma and Mrs. Black, carried away by the adulation of the throngs, attempted to stand, like politicians or returning heroes, but the little foreign cars are not made for such indulgence.

"In front of one dwelling a crowd, larger than usual, had gathered, and Sister Mary Magdalena, thinking it some special ceremony in our honor stopped the car. The crowd, we found, was looking not at us but, to our dismay, at a figure sprawled on the sidewalk. As we paused a large fellow, who seemed, from his tools, to be a window washer, ran up to help. Word quickly spread that an old lady had fallen from the window, apparently while tending her potted plants, as one was lying at her feet. A police officer finally arrived and for a moment the crowd parted, affording us a clearer view of the sad sight. And when reluctantly I looked at the face framed by the white curly wig, wildly askew from the fall, I knew it at once.

"So the Leader was dead—driven by fear and cowardice to disguise himself as the thing he hated the most—an old lady. A fleeting twinge of sympathy touched me and immediately left. Sister Mary Magdalena started the car again and we rode on through the cheering crowds. We had work to do. We had inequities to abolish, rights to restore, changes to adopt. We had to think of our liabilities, of the old men, of what we could possibly do with them without harm to our new government."

The old men, trying again, came out of obscurity, naïvely thinking they would be called into the new government. The old ladies, relenting, but basically relentless, assigned a few to menial tasks. But cleaning the pigeon roosts and mixing up the weather reports on TV was not what the old men had in mind at all. Half scared, half embarrassed, fatalists, they took in the situation, unimproved, and went back to long days in little rooms, re-reading newspapers, or just waiting, sometimes counting silently to ten, then backward. Sometimes they practiced walking young and snappy, and blinking their eyes, vital, interested. It helped pass the time as they waited for the old ladies and their government to be thrown out.

"What kind of government would old ladies form?" wrote Sarah rhetorically, right inside her kitchen cabinet. "The city-state? The philosopher king? Who would be our mentor? Plato, Machiavelli, Locke, Thomas Jefferson, our New England fathers? What utopian model would we pattern our community on? What idealistic failure would we copy?

"Not a damn one. In spite of our foolish whims, our terrible talents, we were practical, hardheaded people. We had just won a war. Our government was down to earth, a kind of democratic demagoguery, parliamentary in practice and with equal votes for all members, forty-nine in number—sixteen from the underground and thirty-three from the bus.

"It was suggested that to show our power we adopt a new flag. Various designs of an irresponsible nature were submitted: an old lady astride the universe with a pigeon on her head; an old lady clinching an umbrella handle, raised in salute. But the more sensible among us voted against the idea. We already had a good flag."

At the first meeting in the basement headquarters, now dubbed Independence Hall (none of the members could stand the height of the Tower) some quick laws were passed.

Restore the parks at once. Dig up the concrete and plant back real trees and flowers.

Return books and music and art to the people. Turn the sound off on TV.

Put cushions on the standpipes.

Restore the benches. Add footstools, warmers in winter, air coolers in summer.

Manufacture furniture taller and with no bottom drawers so older people need not stoop.

Enlarge print in newspapers and books. Even for those not Christian Scientists.

Run the trains again, for God's sake. A civilization built on air travel is dangerous, untenable, and contrary to nature. Join the Train Spotting Club.

Support your local sachet parlor.

Be your own rooster knocker.

Make your pot useful. Don't just sit there watching it. Throw it at the great glass buildings. Help knock down undesirable real estate.

Chop any building over twenty stories in half. Haul the top half outside the city and dump it.

Tear down the wall. Dispense with the gate. Put up
poles to shake against.

Give everybody something to hold on to.

Coordinate the street corners. Allow everyone equal
time.

Tolerate no conflicts of interest in government. Keep
the Vas crooks out.

Stop treating old ladies like old ladies. Treat them like
people.

Restore the courts of justice. Call elderly people to jury
duty.

Drop silly expressions: golden years, senior citizens.

Give everybody the right to jiggle their chinquapins.
Know the left from the right.

Stop paying tribute. Mug the muggers.

Buy our little new car, Dat Nun.

Put some punch in your parking. Knock out a few lights.

Arrange your daisy. Keep your basket full.

Recycle old men.

No paying to pee.

CHAPTER THIRTEEN

"Yeah, business is fine," said the catcher of people, interviewed on TV on his way to work. "Old ladies falling out of buildings all over town." Falling? Yeah, they fell after he pushed 'em. Had he succeeded yet in his ambition to push one out, then run outside and catch her? Not yet, he was sorry to say, too far to run. But with the new law limiting the height of buildings he hoped to succeed soon.

How did he get into apartments and rooms to work? asked the interviewer.

He had a modus operandi, that's how. "I just knock on the door and say, 'Volunteer Window Washers of America, Mom.'"

Did "Volunteer" mean he had no union card?

Look, he had a hell of a union card, bud. "Volunteer" meant he was washing the windows of old ladies free.

Why did he suppose he'd never been caught and arrested?

Arrested by who? He worked in with old ladies. He was their friend. He was doing them a favor. They were lonesome and glad to see somebody. He gave them this new outlook on life. Caught by who? he asked. If *he* with his athaletic training couldn't catch nobody falling, you know the police couldn't catch nobody running. Anyway, when

143

people saw him running up it looked like he was trying to help.

Wasn't he afraid his appearing on these interviews would lead to his ultimate downfall?

Maybe, but like everything else worth while you done, the risk was part of the game. Whatever risk there was, he had to take it in order to give his message to the youth of America: Don't give up, kids. You got a hobby, something bigger than yourself, don't be no lousy quitter on it.

Could he give examples of unusual cases that might be of interest to the youth of America?

All his cases were interesting. If there wasn't something about a case that interested him, he didn't take it. He had this file on all the old ladies in town.

Where'd he get the information for his files? Computers?

Nah, an old lady could break down a computer in no time. She'd have IBM back in the typewriter ribbon business. He had paid, living contacts. One of his sources of information was his contact in the new government. Sure, there were spies in every government. How the hell else did you think a democracy worked?

But some of his best contacts were little kids, especially little girls. Little boys would crap out on you, make up something—"The old lady lives in a broom closet. Her nephew from Long Island has a big ax"—but little girls stay right in there with it. Why? Because they like to tell things, they're building up to be the future old ladies of America. They could tell you every step an old lady took —when she went out, what she bought at the store, what she stole (a stick of butter, a bar of soap), and when she went back home and to what. They ran you a hard bargain on the pay, too, wouldn't settle for no bubble gum or comic book like the boys did; they held out for cash, or maybe once in a while a box of Crayolas. Blackmail the hell out of you if they found out something on you. That's the reason he'd trained his memory sharp and kept his file up here, in his head, where the little girl Youth of America couldn't get to it.

Could he remember some examples from his file? asked the interviewer. Some that had been a particular challenge, perhaps?

He could remember *everything* about his file. Like he just said, that's how he kept ahead. To answer his question: One old dame where she had her stockings hitched to her drawers had caught on the balcony rail, and before she disappeared over the ledge had time to say that though the games had been rough, "They didn't go this far even at Princeton." Jesus, it had kind of shocked him. He had always looked up to Princeton as a place to aspire to send the kid, you know.

One of his most challenging cases, though, had been one with some kind of a pot on her hand. He had to sort of dodge it. Yeah, he could illustrate for the TV. See— follow it with the camera, now, don't lose the camera shot—here's the way he'd had to do it: come around from the left on her and sort of cross hands, like playing the piano. La-de-la-de-la-de-do. She'd been a tough one; he'd got the idea she was trying to tell him how to do it. One of them old dames that has to even boss their own funeral. The case after her had been holding something in her hand too; wouldn't turn it loose. All of 'em want to hold onto something; they hate to let go. That's the reason he always gave 'em his hand. He thought maybe this one had a diamond or one of them old McCarthy buttons or something. Later when she had fell he had seen it hop away and he'd stepped on it quick. A cricket.

Didn't any of the old ladies ever fight back?

Sure. It did you good to see 'em, too. Ain't none of 'em want to go. One when he'd went in her room—a note pinned on the door, unlocked, said, "Come in, ambulance" —had been crawling on the floor by a suitcase, trying to pull herself up. He'd went to the window and started working. At first watching her he'd thought she couldn't make it. Her legs and feet were swollen and wrapped in rags, her hair was falling down in her eyes, but in that traveling outfit she had on, short pajama pants topped with a sweater, she could cover that floor. She was traveling on her rear, not her legs. She got to a chair leg and dragged herself over to the bookcase. From there she made it to the desk and climbed up the desk leg. For a minute it looked like she might topple. She swayed a little, held the desk tight, then she pulled again, and stood straight—a good five feet tall. She shot him a proud, quick look and he clapped his hands. Resting a moment then, she held onto the desk, and he could see how once she might have been a kind of cute-looking old doll.

The desk was where he figured she kept it all: the checks, the cash, the jewelry. Then she opened it—she'd had to stoop a little to do it; once he'd thought the swollen legs would give way—and took out the treasures— six empty glasses cases, three light globes, and two balls of twine. She threw on the floor all but the light globes, lowered herself again down the desk leg, and, shoving her booty along with her, crawled back to the suitcase. She missed it with one of the balls of twine and he came over to pick it up. He stuck it in a corner of the suitcase next to the artificial flower arrangement—one beat-up looking daisy—and the woven basket, raveling, but full of ball-point pens and a catcher's mask.

"And from the ambulance order on the table by all the pills I seen she was packing to go to the hospital."

She'd been game, all right. Even with the sick legs she'd scratched and kicked and put up a hell of a fight at the window. Sure, he'd waited till she finished packing. Suppose something she'd needed bad at the hospital had got left out?

It was cases like these—another had fought back strong as a man—that made the work interesting—a challenge. Most wasn't a challenge though, as much as just plain n-u-t-s, like the one he'd just been on.

CHAPTER FOURTEEN

"You know how some old ladies sneak out and scribble on the walls at night," he said. "'Drop dead. Kill the pigs. The Pope should settle down and marry a nice Italian girl.' All them obscenities? They're all over town, in the lobbies, on the stairways, by the elevators. You may think delivery boys do it, or college professors, well-wishers of the world, but it's old ladies." He'd seen plenty of 'em at it, scratching on the walls in the dark. "Yeah, they're even doing it on the subways now, laying it on to the youth of America. They say it's to keep their identity."

Well, this old lady had all the walls of her room covered with scribbles. "Some old ladies give up," he said. "Just sit there like lumps, waiting, and don't write nothing interesting on their walls. Just who to call if they crap out; some of 'em have a whole list of numbers, trying to impress you, like all these people gonna cry their eyes out. Others just have their nearest kin, which is usually the police number, or they write something like, 'Put in my teeth if I die in my sleep. They're under the pillow.' Or 'Somebody please take care of the cats. The sick one's named Little Boy Blue.' Some have the addresses of all the Schrafft's restaurants jotted down, along with a list of other free toilets around town: 'If you can't make it to Bonwit's, stop at the Met or the zoo.'

"All negative, negative. You come away from a job like that thinking, Why can't people have a cheerful outlook on life?"

Before he knocked that day—Volunteer Window Washers of America, Mom—he'd felt sort of low. He'd just finished a job—messy room, old lady crying, the walls peeling and dirty. He had thought it was going to be an interesting case on account of the challenge of the wheel chair. He'd done plenty of canes, of course, and walkers and crutches were a pushover—just wrap 'em around their necks—but he hadn't done a wheel chair yet. For days he'd been looking forward to it, figuring out his modus. Should he take her out of it or throw out the whole chair? How could he get it over the flowerpots in the window? They all had flowerpots—geraniums, wilted violets—cluttering up the windows. What worried him the most, though, was what if the old lady had one of them fancy battery-type chairs that ran itself? How could he stop it and push at the same time? Chasing the wheel chair around the room would look ridiculous for a businessman.

Well, the whole thing had turned out a disappointment, too easy. The old lady had just give up after he got the brakes off. Doom and gloom all the way. Then he had come into this room he was talking about now. Not that the room itself, with the day bed, a bureau, a refrigerator, a sink showing, was much different from the others. It was what the old lady had done with it. The best way he could describe it, there was life in the room.

First there was the key machine, but he'd been expecting that from the little girl watcher's report. "Unusual? What's unusual about it? Lots of old ladies got key machines now. Invincible makes them. Nah, it ain't electric. Looks like a baby organ. You sit on a stool and work it with pedals, like a wind instrument. Got kind of a keyboard with all them different slits and knobs and buttons to it. You play it and combine the different slits to get the different notches on a key. Yeah, the pedal has a lot to do with how deep the notches go. Like loud and soft on the organ, this is narrow and deep. Remember the old Roxy with the mighty Wurlitzer coming out of the pit, everybody singing 'I scream, you scream, we all scream for ice cream'? And the fellow up there at the console pumping away on the black and white keys?" Well, that's how the key machine was. Done in a nice, dark mahogany.

The old lady had shoved it up near the wall and it was on the walls that she had really gone to town. The minute he'd seen all the blue and green and yellow and red scribbles, done in this colorful Crayola style, his spirits had picked up.

On the wall opposite the door as you entered was *The History of the Banishment*. That's where the key machine was, in a corner kind of. On the wall on the left was *The Story of My Life*. Sometimes the two stories kind of ran together, on account of she'd started her *Life* a long time before the *History*. Chapter 1, "I Am Born in West Newton, Mass.," began at the left of the door as you went in and Chapters 2, 3, 4, 5, 6, 7, "I Am Christened by My Father, the Pastor in the Unitarian Church; I Grow and Grow; I Visit My Uncle in South Carolina: My Melons Are Swelling; Off to Prep School with Janie and Joanie and Tippy; We Win at Hockey: Tippy Was Magnificent; The Yale Prom with Josh: 'Boola Boola' Was Glorious." All of these swung on around the bookcases with old Josh, a home-town boy Papa must have paid to invite her, in there big in bright red. When he met old Tippy, though, one look at her racing down the hockey field in her glorious black bloomers had put the X on Miss West Newton: Now I realize I am plain. But the old girl didn't give up.

Get a load of Chapter 8 over the Shakespeare set, the little girl watcher had told him. For a minute he'd been embarrassed to read anything but the title: "My First Love Affair." He figured maybe she'd been too friendly with old Joanie and Janie and Tippy back there in prep school. Like maybe after the hockey game they used to go to bed and play like they were sleeping, and they were getting nooky all the time. Or maybe after the disappointment of the dance, she'd gone out to get her Boola Boola back. Then he read it.

"It was love at first sight," she'd written. "The moment he lifted his tiny face [Jesus, he'd thought, this kid is too little for the old lady; she's fallen for a dwarf] with his darling black head close to mine [Christ, it's a jig, he'd thought. The old lady's given up Joanie and Janie and Tippy and Joshie for this dwarf jig] my heart stirred." Then came the joker line: "The first time he sat on my finger—"

He thought he hadn't seen it right. The one window was at the back of the room and looked out over a alley, making the room kind of dark, one reason she might have tried to spruce it up with the Crayola job. Or maybe she was one of those old dames that thought she could write a better story than was already in the books. Anyway, when he went to work on the window he'd left his bucket of water in the middle of the room so he could come back and keep up with the continued story. Like if he happened to be at home he watched the stories on TV. He went back and read the line again. He'd seen it right the first time.

Want to know who her first love affair was with?

A chickadee she met in the park one day. Jesus. He couldn't believe it. Cleaning on the panes, he kept thinking: A blue jay or a robin, okay, he could understand. But a chickadee. How had she managed it? Did she go to the park each day and they met in this particular tree, like a love nest? Had she done it like with old Janie? He'd got all excited thinking about it. Who had sat on whose finger first? Was this the first time for both of 'em? What had *Mrs.* Chickadee thought?

Over his shoulder, as he worked, he could see the names of other, middle chapters. *The Year I Won* (she'd beat out a fairy as president of the Library Club). *I March for Women's Rights. The Time I Almost Married* (the son of a bitch, one of them M.I.T. dopes she'd met on a protest march, had found out about the chickadee). That had hit her hard for a while and, scribbling down the wall toward the window, she'd flown off the Crayola with some high-falutin negative shit. She wasn't no hot speller—his kid could beat her—like the -ibles and the -ables gave her trouble, and the *i*'s and *e*'s where the *c*'s came in. But her capital letters and her question marks were as good as he'd seen on any wall.

"What Has My Life Really Meant? Have I Fully Met My Responsibilities to the Hungry, Homeless, Helpless, the Less Fortunate Than I? Have I Done All I Can for My Black, Mexican, Indian, and that New Name, Chicano, Brothers and Sisters? Have I Helped the Ghetto Children, the Migrant Workers, the Helpless Animals of This World? Have My Pet Projects Come to Naught: Free Teeth for Everyone? Free Spays for All, including Cats and Dogs? Have I Seen Justice Done? Have I Stood Up for the Rights of All? Have I Contributed All I Can Financially? Have I Done Enough Ever?"

Then she had done some nifty figuring on her bank statement, under the picture of Mama and Papa on snowshoes in the White Mountains. She hadn't ever been no millionaire, but the next chapter said *NO*, and she was back in business on the wall by the bed. *I Go to Albany Again to Protest: Quit Soring the Horses. Stop Killing the Baby Seals. I Am Mugged in the Hall—Down but Not Out. I March Against the War. I Go to Jail. I March Against the Jail. I Am Mugged on the Stairs. I March Against the Muggers.*

Now and then she would make like an editorial. "All is not well in our government. Even with our resolve to keep the vote equal, to preserve proportional representation, we have made the discovery we wished to avoid—the need for a head. Discord over who this should be has broken out in our ranks. And while, of course, it would seem a natural assumption to most that I would be the logical one to lead—I had the keys, I had found the underground, I had the background—I had hoped to share the leadership with my black sister, Elizabeth. It had been my wish that we could govern together.

"But alas, the ladies of the Parliament have not yet been freed of their prejudices. Have we not been through enough together—humiliation, danger, indignities, banishment; must we still ask what color is my sister? Have we not learned that no one is treated differently under the tyrant? Have we not been debased enough already without debasing ourselves? What calamity must further befall us before we act like sisters and humans?"

Then she'd follow directly with something like "Dump Nixon, Dump Rocky."

In all the later chapters he'd noticed there was often

a comment about the little girl watcher. "I was feeling a bit tired today—I marched to City Hall—and that charming child helped me up the stairs. Reminded me a bit of Joanie.

"The little girl Angy polished my key machine today. Is going to look after me, she said, and insisted on going through my trunks and notebooks for me. Accepted pay reluctantly. Finally consented to take it for her Girl Scout troop. A remarkable child. When Sister Mary Magdalena stopped by, she gave Sister quite a few pointers on the care and maintenance of the little car. Sister was impressed—for once in her life—and I thought more than a bit shaken."

All around the room in spots too small for chapters she had written notes to herself. "Invincable went down again today. Buy." This was running sideways up the wall by "Look up what to do when your partner raises you to four spades, you having inadvertently counted several clubs as spades." And she had the whole bridge game laid out on the wall. She was North. He had caught it in a minute. Play your ace to the opponent's king there, dummy, then finesse your red queen.

By the time he was polishing off the window she had finished a new one over by the door opposite from Chapter 1. "Live in a retirement village where all are the same age, with no youth, and probably no different colors? No, thank you. A hole in the ground is cheaper, and probably more interesting." Then she started on something else. She would write a few words, then look at me working. I couldn't see what she was scribbling now but I figured it was about me, that I was inspiring her with the fine way I was cleaning. Maybe she was putting me on the wall: The Most Memorable Window Cleaner I Have Ever Known. So I give it an extra shine and called her over to the window to inspect it.

"Lean over and take a look," he'd said. "You ain't had this window cleaned since you graduated from Radcliffe, Chapter 10, over by the shell collection. How you ever magna cum-ed with that crazy spelling and that dirty window beats me. You got books you stole from the library the year you last had this window cleaned. But look at it now. I'm doing you a job you won't get nowhere else."

And he had waited for that grateful, appreciative look to come on her face. Like the dawn when he'd been cleaning windows all night, alone away up there somewhere, humming a little Bach, and looked up, and there was the dawn. Give him a funny feeling in the stomach. Yeah, too many pizzas could do it, too.

Finally she had made a big dot with her Crayola like she had finished the chapter. Then she had come over to the window. And funny thing, he had hated to do it almost. "Lots of old ladies who live alone get humped up and shrunken sideways," he said. "Don't take care of their physical appearance. They start doing things with their mouth, chewing their lips, going click, click, click.

But this one had kept herself up. No looker, all right, like she'd said in Chapter 7, and the mugging hadn't helped any, but the marching had kept her on her toes. She still had a nice chest you wouldn't expect on an old dame on a slope, and stood straight and erect in them orthopedic shoes she'd had to get. I'd say working at some desk had broadened her a little in the rear: but that could have been from setting on the standpipes."

Her mouth was firm and ready to smile. From all that Do Unto Others crap, he hadn't picked her for a smiler. She stood there a moment, one hand on the window sill, one hand flung out, girlish. Then that grateful, expectant look had come on her face, like she'd seen something too good to be true, like same as the time (Chapter 14, back of the lamp) when carefree, only forty-three, she had had the great opportunity to take that bus ride down the Greek coastline. And there it had been, even better than she'd ever dreamed, Cape Sounion, hangout of the god Poseidon, Olympic swimmer of that day. Along the road redbud and yellow mimosa had been in bloom, and red poppies where the old man had got his dope. Offshore islands and hills piled up behind the road, and one small blue harbor after another—all so beautiful she had cried.

Watching her now, he hesitated, thinking about Mr. Chickadee out there, waiting with his tiny upturned face and her never showing up, not sending no note even. He read what she'd written above the little marble-top table, the only thing she hadn't sold from the old manse in West Newton to keep up the do-good bit.

"Have I spread myself too thin, have I tried to do too much? Did I have too much fun? Am I holding on Too Long? What is there in the heart of an old woman—and of course I'm not all that old; Tippy was a year older— what is there that keeps her going? Is it greed of life? Am I greedy for life?"

Yeah, you're too greedy, he thought. You should have let some of them other old ladies get in the act. Like back there in Chapter 16 when you enrolled in Key School you should have stayed with those more your age. Instead of putting yourself forward like that with Eddie and Arthur and Louie. When you were *Relieved of Your Position* (boy, were they ever glad to get rid of you) you should have retired gracefully instead of fighting the Leader. You shouldn't have carried all that hatred in your heart.

He got ready to shove her over the sill—anything he despised was an old lady, greedy for life, with hatred in her heart—when he saw the last thing she had written on the wall. "Give up, jerk. Do you think we came through the Banishment to be defeated now?"

It had made him boil. It was negative. It was un-American. The old lady was still in there fighting and she wanted *him* to give up. He started to push again—Alec's was the name of the gym, kids, Alec's—and the old lady reached out for something to hold. In the corner was the hockey stick old Tippy had given her in that victory celebration in 1914, back in Chapter 6, the time they had clobbered old Abbott on Field Day. But she didn't need no hockey stick now. Before he could get the old lady off her feet, the little girl watcher Angy grabbed her hand, and they held on together.

Disgusted, he had taken his bucket and left. Sure, he'd had to pay the kid blackmail, plenty. The crappy kid had been hiding there all the time. Yeah, behind the key machine, I scream, you scream. He knew now she and the old lady were both Commies. Probably in the same double-crossing bloc. Three or four old ladies he did a week were Commies. They always gave themselves away somehow—not wearing no flag, marching against the war, using that red Crayola, making them dirty remarks about the Pope and Princeton.

Yeah, that was the first time he had ever failed—that they'd lived to tell the story. It meant he had to be more careful now. Nah, he wasn't afraid of the news media giving him away. The media was strictly neutral. It meant he had to quit getting soft, fooling around with them humane ideas the old lady was trying to spread. Give up? Hell no. He was due on a new job now. From the file given him by his new government contact it ought to be one of the most interesting cases he'd had.

CHAPTER FIFTEEN

After a hard day on the job she spent a lot of time looking out the window; if he passed on the other side of the street she would spot him easy. Leaning out, she could watch the kids playing stick ball on the street, dodging and screeching as they raced to first base, the clump of green shrubbery under her window. Over in the park she could see the people crowding the benches and admiring the real trees, dropping litter like in the old free times.

While she'd been looking for him the others in the government had got all the choice apartments with the nice glass lookouts on the busy streets, but hers, on a seedy side street, provided a restful scene after a tiresome day at the office with everybody wanting an appointment, calling at the last moment demanding prime time. She had to say, "Corner of Broadway and Eighty-sixth Street, 5:30 P.M. Saturday? Try again in three months. Greenwich Village? Any corner? All booked for two years."

The trouble with people these days, Marge pointedly told Miss Arvin, her ambitious, wren-tailed assistant, was that they wanted everything too quick; they didn't know what it was to work and to wait for something like she did. That was the difference between her and the young

THE BANISHMENT

Jesus cult hippies who wouldn't know him if they met him on the street: they wanted to jump right into business without the experience of waiting. All of her life, as a child even, singing and sweating and giggling at the revival meetings, she had been waiting. I will come, I will come, he had said. Wait for me, I will come, Marjorie Jo. "I know you will when you have time, hon," she said. "I'll wait. Nobody will ever take your place with me." And busy as she was now in her government position she still awoke each morning with the same old sense of expectancy: Today, today, this is the day. Everywhere she went on the job, checking complaints, inspecting suggested openings, she was on the alert. If he passed, or called to her from the other side of the street, she would be ready.

"It has sure kept you young, Marge," people said. One added: "You have sure kept your youth running around like that, popeyed, waiting for him. Living in those lousy rooms near Broadway has built up your physique, girl; climbing up and down those flights of stairs has paid off. Keep on keeping on, Marge." In former days when she had stayed indoors too long, something inside her said, He will come, you might miss him, run, run, perhaps it is he, and she had to be out on the trail again, looking, waiting. "Charge that nut extra for using the elevator so much," a landlord would order, so she would walk up and down the four or five flights, strengthening her legs

166

and leaving her arms trim and firm from carrying the flag and the signs.

Her job as Street Corner Coordinator in the new reform government required that she refrain from active practice but her duties entailed constant field work, and on the street she was not forgotten. "When are you coming back to us, Mad Marge?" On location, in any part of the city, somebody from a street corner would recognize her from the old days and call out, "It's not the same without you, Marjorie Jo. The young Jesus boys will never be like you." It would set her blood racing again, and with her gray hair swinging radiantly free like Lassie's, the telltale bald spot of middle age barely visible, she would long to pace up and down and unfurl the flag, to walk fast down the block, turning her head from side to side like a model or Miss America. But, remembering her government position, she would confine herself to a prudential, presidential wave, holding the fingers apart, a trifle higher, a moment longer, than necessary.

Dispose of Your Business Holdings was a legislative ultimatum. Regarding this she had gone for advice to Miss Irene, sales supervisor in the cosmetic business, her means of support. "Sure, I'd take the job, Marge." Miss Irene was bushy-haired (knew how to thin it, though) and married to a cook who went to Brooklyn at 5 A.M. (sometimes she got up, sometimes not). Pretty once, she was Chicago born; men still looked. "We at Beauty Tone can't stand in your way. In fact, I think we can make a tie-in here. Confidentially, every product on the market needs a little tie-in, Marge."

"I don't need it," said Marge. "He will come."

"Yeah, and when he does he's going to have to face it, Marge. Corners don't get the crowd they did on his previous trip. There're more people wanting corners now than there are people to watch 'em perform. TV and LSD have done it. Sit-ins and take-overs have cut into the business. Everybody's in the act. You got to have a sideline now, too, something extra going for you. This new hair spray—"

Spurning the offer, Marge had turned in her cosmetic bag. Though respected and renowned for her integrity on duty, she could not bring herself to part with the flag and the signs—were they not her youth, her very life?— and instead had hidden them in her room. Often at night, full of a fiery urge, she draped Old Glory across the bed while she watched TV. The shades drawn, she could not resist a fling at the forbidden routines—pace, pivot, reverse. At the office, she was all business, keeping Miss Arvin in line and holding daily pep talks with her field workers who reported for their posts and lists of clients. She herself took the tough spots, insisting on strict adherence to the book. She had trouble with young people; they did not want to make an appointment. Wanted to squat with their homemade jewelry and leather belts without no appointment. "The only appointment I'll give you is to have your hair cut and your face washed," she told them. She kept 'em straight. "Marge certainly keeps her appointments straight," they said enviously in the Parks Department where once they had scheduled two parades running headlong into each other. "Boy, I'd hate to buck up against old Marge without a reservation. Imagine bucking up against old Marge without no reservation and all that goddam integrity sticking out. Poor Herman G. Turner," they said.

On one occasion, Marge, checking locations, had refused position to Herman G. Turner, who had foolishly claimed a reservation he had not cleared with her.

"Listen," she said, blocking his access to the corner. "You have to wait in line to be the only nut on a corner of Broadway, mister. Look at these other three corners. See the puppet lady? Makes members of the English royal family, and the President; you do it by squeezing your fist. See the elderly man sawing at the violin? Juilliard graduate, kicked an old lady who said, 'Squeak, squeak,' at him right in the teeth. See the two boys burning draft cards that on closer inspection probably say Eat at Hu Lee's Upstairs Chinese Restaurant? Well, they've all had their reservations for months. Why, I know one lady had a hibiscus plant and she tried to control the day it would bloom. Just something she ordered from the back pages of the New York *Times* with two other plants that said Water Me. Boy, she worked on that plant till she was batty, trying to get it to bloom on the day she could get a reservation. Called me up and said, 'Marge, don't laugh at me now, but can you accommodate me? How about three weeks from now?' 'Sorry, Ella V.,' I said, 'not a chance. There're too many other fine people on the waiting list.' So you see," she told the man, "it ain't easy. Before I took over the job it was even harder. A retired bookie had the concession, an old ex-pinball machine man, ran it like a racket. Had to bribe him to get a stand, then pay protection. He had a stop watch he used on you. 'Hurry, hurry, your hour is up.' Sometimes after you'd dragged the flag and the signs you found another fellow had paid more and got the spot. Graft."

"Marge is right," said a bystander. "It was much worse in the old days. Marge has extended hours. She brings some system to it."

"Unlike her assistant, Miss Arvin, Marge has risen from the ranks," said another. "She has put her integrity and her know-how into it."

"Well, I'm not bragging," she said, "but when the new government called me in they said, 'Pardon us, Marge, we are not unaware of your long and famous career, of the fact that as a child with yellow bangs and sashed skirt you were apprenticed to the streets' finest teachers. To wit, Mother Alexander, who, all the while preaching a rapid hell-fire sermon, could stop traffic with her graceful turns and flourishes. Nobody, we understand, could execute the pivot at the corner like Mother Alexander, seeming to leave but never going, appearing to vanish but always returning. We are aware that you also had instruction from Livingston and Todd, catering more to the dialectic taste—Was Jesus the father of Karl Marx? —though not above opening their pants to hold the crowd when it grew restless, or offering small balloons and needle threaders.

"'This glorious background has not eluded us, Marge,' they said, 'or your fine work in the camp and on the march. But for the record we have to give you this civil service exam: Can you stand for hours not only on the sweet spring days and in the good fall weather that says, "Regard the sky, Live, live, live," but can you take it with a hundred-degree heat pounding on your head? Do you know all the protective awnings in town? The ten-cent cups of coffee? Can you deliver a spiel without losing your breath and your audience? Can you shift your weight to ease your varicose veins? Can you keep a hard-boiled egg warm in your pocket, can you cuddle a cup of coffee with a leaflet in one hand and the flag in the other? Can you still turn being a freak into an advantage like you did on the turnpike? Can you wait, wait, wait, without dying?' 'Listen,' I said, 'I always made it to those corners irregardless of the weather.' 'Give the kid her own corner,' people said. 'The kid's won the right to her own corner. The kid's a natural for the job.'"

She stood firmly in the path of the man; she kept him off the curb. Pushy-lipped, he persisted. "You got the big mouth, all right," he said. "You got the training with the patter and the spit. You got the proper crazy look back of them thick glasses. But you ain't getting away with this. We been planning this for months. The day I got the reservation I rushed home and said, 'Look, kids, we got the reservation,' and we worked up a real little act. The kids can go like different birds. We live in New Jersey near a swamp, see. Yeah, it's lonesome, but it's cheap and my kids can watch the birds. They ain't too many interesting things to do in a swamp, you know. I'm an actor by trade so I'm naturally home most of the time. 'The house ain't big enough for us all,' says the wife, 'try the swamp.' So I go out to the swamp a lot. Sometimes to kill the monotony me and the kids put on plays. I'm not saying they're like Broadway but I've taught myself to use different voices talking to the trees and the animals. I can imitate the fox and the bay-breasted warbler. I can call out To-Who-O and get the answer from the other side of the swamp. I can talk tall as a aspen tree and low as a mud turtle. You ever seen the diagram on a turtle's back, lady, when he's stopped in the path, head stuck out, listening to you? Down the middle are diamonds in black and on each side is a band, orange-colored sometimes. Kathleen, my oldest, has made some drawings of it. Pass out the drawings to the people, sister."

Sister, embarrassed and beginning a bosom, passed out the drawings; deserters from the puppet lady came over for samples to add to the royal family. Marge, casing the newcomers for possible troublemakers, thought she saw Miss Arvin, her little wren tail raised like a weapon as she butted through the crowd. Had the government sent her out as a spy? wondered Marge. Had they guessed about the flag and the signs? She wiped her glasses and looked again; if Miss Arvin had been there she had now left, but Herman G. Turner, in the gutter, over which Marge had no jurisdiction, was still holding forth.

"Sometimes the pond near us floods over and we got acquainted with a young beaver family that way; came right up to the back door on a little raft they'd made. Twigs laid just as nice. 'Look, kids, how nice the beavers have laid the twigs,' I said. And my son here learned to lay them twigs, too. But it's the birds my kids get to know the best. When they're mating the birds do these nuptial dances. Minuet and square dances are favorites, and ducks do mock flights on the water. Some birds just nod up and down in a kind of wing display, like people. You know, nod, peck, nod, peck, run off, hurry back. The kids watch 'em and practice it. The wife here's made these costumes that flip, flap like wings. The kids go way out into the swamp to find the feathers for 'em. It makes you jumpy till they get home. 'Are the kids home yet from the feather hunting?' I say to the wife. 'It's time the kids were home.' Sometimes I go out to meet 'em and they come back with all kinds of feathers. Junie, hon, show the people your new speckled bird

173

dance. Junie found these feathers all by herself under one of the new highway machines that are coming in. Show 'em, baby, like we practiced at home."

The little girl, the plumes drooping down her neck now, said, "You do it, Daddy," and pushing her toes against the curb, the feathers, as she bent, rising like a cock's on mount, tried to pull him back to his place on the corner. The wife, maker of the costumes, sewer of the horny seams—try it on feathers sometime, her eyes said, hard—had stood still watching. A spectator held out his hand to help; one of the feathers loosened from the little girl's wing and clung to his fingers; he put it in his pocket with the drawing of the turtle's back, and pulled. Marge blocked the way again; Herman G. Turner retreated to the curb. "You show 'em then, Wallace. Show 'em your crippled-goose dance." But the boy, suddenly shocked by the whole thing (My God! My God!), hung back, his head pointed west, toward Jersey, and the man danced a few steps alone on the curb. The dance was not his art, talking was his art, the sharing, the airing of the word, and seeing his children embarrassed, eyes fixed on the other corners, he tried to reverse, lost balance, and fell awkwardly. From the curb Marge watched him, unmoved. Rising, he turned on her again. "You don't give a damn whether a bird dances or not."

"Listen," said Marge, "when I was a kid I didn't have no chance to watch a bird dance. I had a hard life, mister. 'Your father will never be any good,' my mother said to me, outside the big tent, and I was just ten years old. 'He has not got the knack with the crowd,' she said. 'Look at him, he can't even pee straight. He'll always be a two-bit preacher in a one-horse town. You go, Marjorie Jo,' she said, 'and make something of yourself. Your talent for carrying the crowd with you will far outweigh the fact that you can't see two feet in front of you without your glasses. Unfortunately I have to stay with Papa,' she said. And she apprenticed me to Mother Alexander. Believe me, it was no bed of roses. I was out on those corners from dawn to dark. I wasn't fooling around in no swamp on no feather hunt. 'Do the pivot,' ordered Mother Alexander. 'Do the abrupt repeat. Stick out your hands, like at the Supper. Pull 'em back. Pull up your socks. Uncross your eyes. Hold up your shoulders. Balance your butt. Pull in your neck. Try to look bright. Put down that Bible, it's too confusing. Say you got the word personally that he's coming. Stick to that.' And I told 'em about Jesus. 'Do you believe that crap you're spouting, kid?' people would ask. 'Of course I believe it, it's my life,' I said. Now get off," she told Herman G. Turner. "The corner is reserved."

He made another abortive effort to gain the corner, took the gauge of the eyes behind the thick glasses, then decided to go. "I'll get even with you, lady. Come on, June baby."

"Let's stay, Daddy, and see the other corners." Hoping

175

to win him over, the little girl flopped her feathers like
an old bird, bemused. "Let's watch the puppet lady."

"After I been thrown out? Nothing doing. I got some
pride."

Sullenly they had followed him; the wife had walked
behind, not meaning to catch up now, or ever; this was
just one more thing that had come between them. Fingers sore to the bone, sewing the feathers, stinking sometimes, him home in the way, all day, and now this, no
reservation.

On the job, keeping order, Marge usually felt strong
and important. But she had felt bad seeing those kids
straggle down the street in their feathers. Now why
couldn't that spoilsport let 'em stay and watch the other
corners? Once, thinking of the dismal, dank future, the
kids clamming up on him, sitting silently on the edge of
the swamp, the man shouted back at Marge: "I cleared it
at the office, I tell you. I did clear it at the office, Junie."

People on the corner watched. "Junie is not answering,"
said one. "She's gazing back at the puppet lady." "Maybe
Mom can learn to make puppets for the act," said another.
"How about that, June and Bonny Prince Charlie."

"June is too young for Prince Charles," said someone,
approving. "More suitable, Kathleen, the turtle-back artist."

"Marge should have let him have the corner," said the
first person, still watching. "Give him some prestige with

the kids and his old lady." "Nah, give 'em a corner and
the next thing you know they want the whole block.
Whole goddam swamp come in wanting a block. Beavers
be all over the place with them twigs."

"Where's the guy that's supposed to have the corner,
Marge?" asked the first man, twisting a feather in his
hand. "Where's the guy that's in the book?"

"Yeah, why ain't he here, Marge, if you're so particular?"

"Listen, don't blame it on me," she said. "I like to
have some fun, too. I have a heart. 'Marge,' Mother Alexander used to say to me, 'you may have been standing
behind the door when they passed out the brains, but
you sure got a heart, kiddo, you got some real fun in
you. However, responsibility to your public comes before all else.'" Marge removed her heavy-lensed glasses
and, wiping them, blinked with blind integrity into the
crowd. "The corner is reserved for Alfred E. Atkins."
She put back on the glasses. "It's written in the book at
the office."

"Then where is he? The way corners are scarce now,
he should be here to claim it. I think the bird man is
right. The corner is legally his."

"Marge has made a mix-up in the office and demeaned
a man before his family. She has hurt little Junie, and
this lovely feather from the yellow-throated warbler."

"The yellow-throated warbler is no denizen of the

swamps," said another. "He is southern and a habitant of large evergreens. It is a feather of the yellow-breasted chat that Marge has demeaned."

"Listen, I have not demeaned any damn feather," said Marge. "It is the fault of my assistant, Miss Arvin, who has given me the wrong name for the corner."

"Do not lay it on to the absent Miss Arvin," one said, offended.

Adept at sensing the fickle, changing mood of the crowd (Livingston and Todd had known just when to button up, at what psychological moment to jerk back the balloons), Marge had felt that most of the people had turned against her. Hurrying back to the office, she searched the books again. She found the entry for the day, the area, the block, the corner. The name, entered in Miss Arvin's determined upright script, was *Herman G. Turner*. She sat a long time, quietly staring at it, bringing her glasses down close to the page. Then she put the book away. All afternoon she watched Miss Arvin's bold little posterior, packed as tightly as though for mailing, dart between her Assistant's Desk and the Office Upstairs. That night, full of a strange relief, she got ready. She paced the floor and perfected the pivot. She draped Old Glory on the bed. She shook the wrinkles from her costume, a type of Isadora Duncan dancing dress, with sleeves. She made a sign: *Watch for Opening Date.*

CHAPTER SIXTEEN

When the telephone rang that day, though, she could hardly believe the time had come so soon. It had started as a typical morning. In pep meeting her field workers made their customary demands: shorter hours, increased pay, more say in management. Everybody practiced a new blocking technique, stolen from the New York Jets, and dispersed to their respective areas. Things went pretty much on order, phones ringing with last-minute requests for good locations at prime time, and Miss Arvin right on hand hoping to catch Marge in another mistake. It was late in the afternoon when a most unusual thing happened. Absorbed in plans to open a new section on Park Avenue (rich in talent, poorly represented), Marge realized that Miss Arvin had raised her voice over the phone. "You wish to *cancel?*" The prized executive low pitch hit a high-rising note of incredulity. "This afternoon at the northwest corner of 110th and Broadway at five-thirty? Yes, sir, thank you for calling, sir. No, sir, I'm afraid I can't offer an alternate date. We're booked solidly in that neighborhood. Sorry you can't make it, sir."

Even when Miss Arvin distinctly repeated the time

and location, Marge thought the wires had got crossed
with the Parks Department (bicyclists had ridden right
through a performance of *Henry IV*) but Miss Arvin
said positively the call had been for Coordinator; she,
Miss Arvin, would immediately inform the lucky person
next on the waiting list. "Don't trouble yourself, my
dear," said Marge. "How about taking an armful of that
backlog up to Central Files and doing some work for a
change?"

What makes a person in high office embrace the un-
ethical? What steely resolve melts to mush? Marge never
stopped to wonder; she scratched out the name *J. C.
Sakes* and wrote *Designated* in the cancellation before
Miss Arvin, making the trip to Central Files, two flights
up, in record time, was back in the room. In the afternoon she left the office early, presumably for the pro-
posed Park Avenue site.

The September sun was still high and hot when she
arrived at the appointed corner. Blue Charlie, an old-
timer and the two-thirty to five-thirty occupant, was just
leaving with his sandwich sign: *Watch Me Turn Blue.
Skin, Hair, Tip of Toes, As Well as Outer Garments.* He
headed for a bar, puzzled every time he failed. "You can
do it if you try, Charlie," called Marge. How batty could
you get? she thought, then forgot him, busy with house-
keeping. ("Try to make each corner a little bit of home,"
said Mother Alexander. "Don't be such a slob.") First she
unfurled and affixed the flag, a requisite. In a circle she

propped up her signs. She put out Beauty Tone containers of plastic that she could not bear to throw away. "He Will Come," she announced, and was in business.

It was prime time at an A-1 location, in front of a liquor store by a bus stop and a subway stop, with two bars in view. Across the street on the northeast corner a juggler was tossing a sausage and two empty deposit bottles he had found in the garbage; his object was to finally catch the sausage in his mouth, without losing the rhythm. On the southwest corner, by the Broadway bus stop, a woman had two dachshunds she had taught to sing. They wore coats cut down from her crocheted sweaters and when she raised her hand like a baton, the dogs stood on their hind legs and howled; people loved it. "What aria is that?" asked an admirer. "Sounds like something crazy from *The Magic Flute*." On the fourth corner, southeast, was Lady Merle, a registered psychologist, who could cure cats and warts.

A crowd soon gathered, shoppers after the fruit-stand specials, sunners, strollers, students from the university. This was one of Marge's favorite spots, this busy and dangerous crosstown street of the West Side; she had spent some of the happiest hours of her apprenticeship here and it was like coming home now. Many, passing by her corner, stopped to welcome her. Remembered, she swelled with pride, and almost wished Miss Arvin were there to see it all. "There she is," people said when they recognized her. "Mad Marge of the old days."

"Sister, is he coming tonight? Can I take time for a pizza before he gets here?"

"He'll come, all right," she said. "Don't worry, he'll be here."

"Did you say don't worry or don't hurry, sister?"

After the stuffy office work, with the envy and intrigue, and Miss Arvin plotting behind her back, it was great to be on the street again. Near her, pigeons promenaded in the gutter. At the fruit stands people chose their melons as though for life; the thirsty entered the liquor store. As the afternoon passed the dachshunds sang louder, something from Verdi, off key, the juggler nearly swallowed one of the bottles, and Lady Merle, the psychologist, took a live wart, big as a honeycomb, from a Barnard girl's arm. People, feeling the excitement of it—it was wonderful having her back, they kept telling Marge, "You will always be our Marge"—squared the block. A police car arrived and parked down the street by the supermarket. From here the law kept an eye on the corners or stepped in when requested or inclined.

A group of college students emerged from the steakhouse, "$1.49 with Idaho," and crossed the street to Marge's corner. Probably to write her up, she thought, and placed the sign *He Certainly Will* nearer the empty Beauty Tone containers, making a background like New Cinema. Mother Alexander had composed her own colorful brochures to hand out, but Marge had never felt the need for these. It was so simple: he would come and she would know him. "How?" asked one of the students now. It was a routine question, not one she asked herself often, though frequently put to her. During the early revival days they had sung, "I shall know him by the print of the nails in his hand," but she had never thought of the meaning much, it had just been something to repeat and repeat until the sinners, usually old women and children, ran crying to the altar. "Know him?" she countered now. "How can I fail to know him?" How to explain it to those who could not understand! ("It's my business to know him," had been Mother Alexander's answer. "Do I ask you if you know *your* merchandise?")

The students walked on. A woman with a real raccoon sauntered by. A drunk man teetered on the corner and shouted at the little dogs: "Can't you punks sing any better than that?" Then he burped and went on. By the uptown subway exit a crowd gathered in front of Lady Merle, who also read fortunes. Across the street the juggler added a jar of mustard to his act and drew some of the dachshunds' audience from the Broadway buses. When the crosstown buses from Fifth Avenue finally appeared, traveling in packs as though for protection, irate passengers made their exit on the corner by Marge. Late, some walked on fast, but others stopped to look and to listen. A holiday spirit pervaded and Marge felt the old blood tingling. She always responded best to a large crowd and in the heckling now she held her own. "He will come, he will come," she sang, almost gaily. "Just turn out to be a big Jew," said someone, still mad about the buses. "You take his bus, mister," said Marge, "and you'll get there on time. He will come."

"Why doesn't he come on then?" Blue Charlie had left the bar and with his sandwich worn inside out (Temporary Job Opportunities) confronted Marge. "What the hell's keeping him? Got to sit up all night making some corny parable? Some sick fellow got to be raised from the dead? Tell us about it, Marge. Where is he?"

"Oh, he'll come in time," she said, smiling into the crowd. Shopping for entertainment, more people paused at her corner.

"In time for what? Stop pacing, dear, and listen," said Charlie. "I've seen you stand on these corners and grow old. I've watched the few men of the masculine persuasion who were drawn to those once golden bangs turn to others while you waited to play pittypat with him. Why doesn't he *take* time and come on? He's got time enough to supply the multitudes with loaves and fishes, and all that cheap wine. He's got plenty of time for Martha and Mary, and walking on the water, keeping cool, while you sweat it out on the corners."

"I can wait. He will come." She could not be shaken, and Charlie, brooding (Nothing fancy like cobalt, Prussian, ultramarine, or any of the acrylic colors some of the boys wanted; just a pale blue, for God's sake. Was that so much to ask?), went back to the bar. Head high,

Marge began to march back and forth, adding a new
hesitation step she had adopted one year from Miss
Iowa (only a runner-up for the crown, but strong on the
Think Question: "Who do I think is the greatest man in
the world? Why, my daddy"). Catching her confidence,
the crowd began to flow to Marge's corner; making a
quick count, three to every actual two, she estimated
four fifths to be with her. (Once on a competing corner
she had even beaten Mother Alexander's record.) At her
peak now, she passed out the leaflets; she paced trippingly
to the corner. ("The kid is not ready for a corner yet,"
said Mother Alexander, peeved.) She whirled about face
in the old glorious manner. Why hadn't they given it to
the little Iowa girl? she wondered. ("I guess you could
say my daddy is my real boy friend.")

And suddenly, shoved from behind, she felt herself
falling. Straddling the flag, she tried to balance herself,
clutched at her glasses, and lost them. The sickening
sound of glass ground into cement stunned her. A policeman came over. "Quit straddling that flag, lady," he said,
indignant. "You ain't supposed to straddle no flag, you
know. Not on my beat." He went back to the car. Marge
groped blindly on the pavement; there was a flurry of
people passing, then the glasses were placed in her hand.
"Not much left but the frames," a voice said. "You got
tackled from behind, lady. Looked like a real pro did it."
Her hands shaking, Marge tried to put on the glasses,
missed, found the hooks for her ears, then finally found

her ears and her nose. Prisms shot out in all directions. Shimmering crazy quilts danced on the traffic lights. Dazed and dizzy in the shattering sunlight, Marge now felt herself alone; the crowd had dispersed, and through the cracked, quivering lenses she saw why.

There he was, big as life in white robe and sandals. Through the crowds he came, moving with the high calm step of the man accustomed to damp feet, or one who had walked on the water. Through the broken glass his face was blurred but he appeared to look out over the crowd with the eyes of a man who had seen things high and low. Slowly he moved, laying on the hands as people rushed up, reaching out one over the other into the crowd, trying to touch them all.

"Hello, Marjorie Jo." His voice was deep, with a gentle compelling mastery; the voice of a man who could talk to all and any, who got answers when he called. There was something vaguely familiar about it, but had she not always known there would be? Had he not spoken to her each day through the years: I will come, wait. Would she not know that voice anywhere? For a moment now, half blind, and speechless with a perfect joy, she hesitated. What she at first thought must be ecstasy almost gagged her, then she got her uppers back in place. "Oh, hon, you made it," she cried. "Bless your heart, you *came*." She turned to the crowd, arms wide open ("Not too wide," said Mother Alexander. "Space it like a fat soprano"). "Look, look," she cried. "He *came*." Oh, bless, bless, bless, she thought. He *came*. "Yes, join me, sister, join me," he said. "Oh, I will, I will. Oh, thank you for coming." "Come right up, sister, come right up." "Oh, I will, I will." And trembling with triumph, she tried to get a footing in the crowd.

But the crowd had swarmed about him now, and touching here, touching there, benign, beneficent, he was everywhere. "Come right on up, sister," he called. "Where are you? Where are you?" she called back. She tried again and was almost knocked down by the crowd. Stepping back then, she waved the flag; she passed out the leaflets, she pointed to the sign He Will Come, but it had lost its promotional value. There he *was*, hogging the show. Frantically Marge tried again, charging blindly with the flag, putting it on a purely patriotic basis. "Look at Old Glory," she cried. "Watch her wave. The grandest old flag in the world. Support your flag," she called. "Remember our fighting boys." But there was not room in the crowd for the flag to wave, and it curled limply about her neck. She stood back a moment then, watching. He was saying little except "Thank you, thank you," but always he sought the hands, lingering, as though the touch were a gift. Rushing forward, the crowd became a mob.

The humiliation was too much to bear, and pushing with the crowd, using all the strength in her arms and legs, Marge got within earshot. "Your name is not in the appointment book," she shouted. "I was able to make it after all, sister," he called. "I checked in with this young lady from your office." Then the crowd pushed Marge aside. "Wait your turn," said somebody, outraged, and forced her from the corner. Helpless now, she stood, blurry-eyed, on the curb until the crowd pressed back against her. Trying to pivot in the old face-saving method, she pitched forward into the gutter. She lay still for a moment, until, wiping the pigeon droppings from her dress, she stumbled to her feet. Scattering the Beauty Tone containers, she took the flag and the signs and in a haze of sick disbelief crossed the street. Brakes squealed and a driver shouted angrily; she plunged on until she reached the police car. "He's over there disturbing the peace," she said. "He's blocking traffic."

Eyes stinging, ears ringing, she waited. "Marge," a voice from the crowd called, "loan him your flag. Loan him Old Glory, Marge, and they won't arrest him." "Let him bring his own goddam flag," she said, and the police car took him off. "Marge has lost her integrity," said somebody. "It is time for a new Coordinator." But standing there with the signs and the flag, Marge paid them no attention. "So maybe it's not so dignified," said someone, passing. "Maybe your feather puppet does look like old Marge over there. I tell you, you got to hand out a little come-on. You can't get a crowd without it." "I am strictly offended," said another.

Marge hardly heard them. The son of a bitch had *come*, for Christ's sake.

CHAPTER SEVENTEEN

All the way home she thought about it. After she'd climbed the four flights to her apartment and sunk, exhausted, on the sofa, her hands, adjusting her spare pair of glasses, still shook with indignation. Blue Charlie was right. Where had he been on the march back to the city when, eating scraps and swill, they had needed him so? Where were the loaves and the wine and the fishes while she nearly starved on berries and grass and leftover Howard Johnson?

When the doorbell rang she didn't answer, remembering how it used to be. Her heart thumping, her legs quivering—run, run, surely this is the day—she had hurried to meet him. Often her hands had trembled so she could hardly open the door and she had left it ajar for him. Now as the bell rang again she merely called a weary "Come in" and relived the humiliation of the afternoon.

"Volunteer Window Washers of America, Mom." A man entered the room, glanced briefly at the walls, and went at once to the window. For a moment he watched the boys playing, five stories below. Then he began to work silently, efficiently, with evident pride in his skill.

A smudge on one pane worried him and he rubbed at it doggedly. He stood off to regard the result; it failed to meet his standards and he polished again, reaching under and outside, holding onto the sill. In the game below somebody made a hit and ran for base; he saw the boy slide into first, then he rubbed hard again. Quietly he began to hum.

"Want to look, lady?"

Yeah, thought Marge, couldn't find ten minutes to come help them when they were loaded onto the buses and banished from the city. Only one nice fellow had tried to help. But *he* had to wait and come today when she finally had prime time and the crowd with her.

"Lady," said the man at the window, "I said come look."

This time she looked up, arrested by a curious note of impatience in the voice. Her eyes angry, remote, still smarting, she sat very still. "Lady," she heard again, and walked to the window. The light streaming through the polished panes dazzled her. On the glistening glass a kind of halo shone around the man's head—right where she had rushed home and torn off her *He Will Come in '72* sticker.

"Next time cooperate," said the man. "Don't paste nothing on the window. Paste is bad for the glass. And don't wait so long again. It makes my work harder. It cuts me down on the next job."

Stunned by the colossal gall, she remembered all the

THE BANISHMENT

dark days of waiting, fixed up and ready, enduring the
hoots of the crowd—sometimes she had almost died of
shame—but she had known it was worth waiting for.

"I'll come as soon as I get the word," said the window
washer. "Promptness makes good business. Trouble is,
you work up a good business like this, who you gonna
leave it to? Take my kid. He don't want to follow in my
footsteps. He ain't no ball player like them kids outside.
All he wants is to stay home and play the piano. Bach.
That's what I was humming. A fugue."

Wait, wait, wait, and today when she had got the
best spot, beat out all them shitty young Jesus freaks, he
had come and hogged the show on *her* corner, on *her*
time.

"I said Bach, lady. Are you deaf or don't you care for
the classics? Anyway, it sort of makes you wonder what
you're bustin' your brains out for, trying to be the best in
the trade, if your lousy kid don't want nothing of it. The
wife says, 'John, you just have to remember what you
were put in this old world for—to help others. So to hell
with the kid,' she said."

By now he realized she was not listening. "Lady," he
shouted angrily. "I said the kid don't want the business
so I'm gonna wash the windows for the old ladies free.
I imagine they'll put me on the board of directors of an
old folks' home somewhere. Lady."

Marge was still preoccupied.

"I'm gonna clean the windows for all the old ladies in

195

the new government. Got the contract today from that Miss Arvin, my contact in the administration. Now lean out the window, lady, and see a new life open up."

He put down his rag and moved the flowerpot. Gallantly he held out his hand. When he became director of the home he imagined he'd have to do this a lot, kind of maybe bow a little and watch the grateful look like the dawn come on the old ladies' faces. He knew now how he had failed with the old lady on the slope. He should have knelt more. He tried it now, bending his knee, off balance for a moment. Instantly Marge reversed, shifted weight, and as she and her assistants had often practiced in the field, threw him over her shoulder.

The children below called time. Then they moved around the man to the house beyond and continued their game. He had fallen on first base, but lucky, they had found another.

Marge shut the window and straightened out the flag on the bed—loan him Old Glory indeed!

CHAPTER EIGHTEEN

"We've got six million little concrete protectors in storage," wrote the C. P. Manufacturing Company, an affiliate of Unbeatable, in a memo to the president of Invincible. "Our salesmen are out of work. Our factories are closed. Get back the concrete or we're ruined."

"The whole economic system is threatened," said the president, rubbing the knot on his head.

"Yes, sir," said the vice-president. "Here is my report, sir."

"Beauty parlor shares have nose-dived," read the president, "for it is fashionable now to look like an old lady, one of the ruling class. Paper stock, with the large print in vogue, is skyrocketing, but the publishers, forced to use more paper, are broke, as are the dentists and opticians who because of the free glasses and teeth have to adjust their living scale to that of ordinary people."

The president looked up from his reading to find the vice-president watching his knot; he put his hand over it and continued. "The stock exchange may collapse. Darting here and there on the floor, near the curb, under the counter, waving, signaling, the old ladies rule the market. Two fingers on the cane, sell. Three, with the thumb raised, buy. Dow Jones Industrial averages decline daily, the *Times* Ten Selected stocks show irregular gains, growth stocks are stunted, and esteemed brokerage houses have failed. But the sightseeing business is good. Chartered planes and buses converge on the city from all sections of the country with people paying to see the old ladies in action, while the pigeons, blue chips in their beaks, serve as messenger boys and whirl and fly about the stock exchange."

"Get me 500 shares of sightseeing stock," said the president, then read on. "The entire city is full of the sound of fluttering wings again. Even though it appeared that the old ladies had killed off the pigeons, the very thing they wanted to save, somebody had kept back one, as always some nosy Noah will save one of everything who will soon find a mate or make it. Somewhere always, unknown, unheard, unseen, a platypus will be platting his pus, a tyrannicus erectus erecting. And an old lady will find him, and save him."

The president finished the report. "Buy me a thousand shares of platypus. Look into the tyrannicus erectus potential," he said, and went to the knothead doctor, a busy man, not easy to see. "You are stuck with the goddamned thing, that's all," said the doctor. "Quit trying to hide it. Make the most of it. Fortunately I happen to be selling this little knothead battery. You just plug it in. Light up the goddamned thing. Be sure and keep it away from antelopes, though. Hide it in the bottom drawer when you're not using it."

The president hurried back to the Invincible office. "Buy into the knothead battery business quick," he said.

"We *own* it," said the vice-president coldly. "Unthinkable, a subdivision of Redoubtable, a branch of Invincible, *makes* it. It is an offshoot of our electric borer that goes through cement, a favorite of old ladies to plant their damn flowers in the concrete."

"Then corner the bottom drawer market," said the president. "Write a report on it," he added severely, "and leave out the fluttering-wings crap."

"Speaking of bottom drawers, I miss one," people began to say when the report came out. "The unity of the American family is built on the firm foundation of the bottom drawer. Not the middle or the top but the bottom. Little animals have crawled into them and died. Theater and laundry tickets have been tossed into them by determined parakeets and never seen again. A bottom drawer is the only place you can keep certain articles." "What certain articles? Things you don't want me to find?" a wife would ask suspiciously. Then she would ransack her husband's drawers and a real fuss would shape up, after which, of course, he had to rent a safety deposit box at the bank. Making up later, the couple blamed it on the old women.

Grumbling and criticism of the old women, hushed at first, became open and widespread. "How come there's no fires any more?" asked the merchants. "We got to get rid of this stock. This crummy stock has got to move for the fall line." Parents chimed in. "You realize our kid's never seen a real fire? Our kid's deprived. This is a hell of a government, depriving our kid."

And they began looking around, outside the city, for a better government. A regular town had grown up there, people living in the top halves of the tall buildings dumped from the old city. As in former days when people had driven out to see the wall, they now went out to New City, which they soon began to say was the Real City. They said, "Put me down on the waiting list for Real New City"; this became *the* place to live. Boy, was it ever a relief, people said, to get away from a bunch of squabbling old ladies and live under an experienced government again.

"The *New* Committee it's called this time," wrote Sarah, home again to her walls. "Same old faces, same old corruption. But what they say is true, I'm afraid. There are now open quarrels over leadership in our own government."

Those who had entered the city as conquerors thought they should hold more and higher positions than those who had stayed in the safety of the basement underground eating lamb chops, playing with pigeons, and making silly posters. After the long, cruel march back to the city, living off berries and grass, hiding in ditches in daytime, traveling only at night, cautiously, fearfully, singing to keep up their courage, each one felt she deserved to be the real Head. Also there were more of them.

More or not, the newcomers were surely the loudest, said the old ladies of the underground, and they accented newcomers and loudest in an uncomplimentary way. It was *they*, the old settlers, who had had the hardships, remaining where the danger of discovery was ever imminent. They hadn't been out on the road in a nice bus, enjoying the fresh air, taking old-maid pottery lessons. They hadn't been to summer camp, living it up at Howard Johnson's, stealing chickens, and scaring the natives. Sitting around on their rumps playing yoga. They had been underground doing the dirty, dangerous, essential work. They had made the keys and had generously opened the city gate, allowing the others to enter. And they didn't need a bunch of hayseed refugees telling them what to do, either.

"Who went out, disguised, in danger, and brought back news?" said the scout. " 'Make Mrs. Ryan the Head,' they all said, 'even if she does look like a man.' "

"Listen," said the poster makers. "We've made our art one of the fastest selling commodities on the market. We should be Head and we got the posters that say so."

"You maybe can make those kindergarten posters," said the sachet lady, "but you sure can't read the handwriting on the wall. Who here but me do you think is the right color? Who put the little rocks back in the supermarket chickens? Who made the firebombs? Who kept the beer and the Bible flowing? Who kept life worth living?"

"Us," said the grass growers.

"There is no doubt who is Head," said Sister Mary Magdalena. Had she not been the one who had crawled under the bus that night and pulled out the gasket that had stalled the bus on the mark, almost as precisely as a moonshot—one of the secrets learned in that sweet Italian summer, secrets known only, thank goodness, to two people—and that sympathetic little innkeeper who had later turned out to be acquainted with the sweet child Angy. Had not her technology made the Dat Nun the fastest, most popular small car on the market? "There is no doubt at all who is Head," she said. But she did mean God.

"It is purely an academic question," wrote Sarah, who had long ago settled it with her New England conscience. "If Elected I Will Serve." She called up Eddie and Arthur and Louie. "Come on over and be Head with me."

The boys met to talk it over. "We've got to tell Gran," said Eddie. He hated it most of all. Somehow he had always felt closer to Gran than the others had. Always there had been that extra something—greed, curiosity?—that had drawn them together. He had stayed by her side day after day at the machine. He had showed her how not to get the key dye under her fingernails, and now he was chosen to break the news to her. "Jesus, we failed old Gran, the first thing she ever asked us." He went to her, wishing he were still an irresponsible boy in vocational school. "It's like this, Gran. We've got a better thing going. We're moving to New City. Greater Opportunity is there, Gran."

For friendship's sake he reminisced about the good old days in seminar: the time he, Eddie, had produced the key that would unlock *anything* and destroyed it immediately—"It just wouldn't have been right to keep it, Gran"; the way when they parted they always said "G.O." instead of "Good-by" or "God bless you." But neither of their hearts was in it; the easy give-and-take of key-making was gone. He had failed her and they both knew it.

Insurrection among the old ladies spread into civil war. Finally in convention in the basement headquarters of Independence Hall, two rival factions picked their respective candidates for Head: Marjorie Jo, back in good governmental standing for having pushed the pusher, and Sarah. A fair amount of low-down politicking followed but at the polls a few miffed pigeons, disenchanted with both sides, stuffed the ballot box and nothing was decided.

Listening on the stairs, the vice-president of Invincible made his move. He had seen it coming, had hastened it by originating some of the criticism of the old ladies, and had written in a secret report: "From the very moment I left the basement door open for the old keybiddy to get in I knew I had something going for me. All the time that knot-head was saying, 'Make a report, make a report,' I was working. It was expensive lugging in the lamb chops from New Jersey and my father expecting the same price as in the open market, even though they were second quality. 'Listen, Papa, when I am the Leader you will be paid.' 'Leader, my foot,' said my father, 'you couldn't lead a sheep if it wasn't in chops. You didn't even stand up for the pigeon in the factory when you knew he should have had the job. I'm ashamed of you,' he said, and he and my mother talked of it in bed when they couldn't sleep. 'We have a son who will not stand up.'

"But look at me now, Mama and Papa, how tall I am standing. Surely I must be the next Leader. I go now to address the convention."

"Tippy, tippy, tippy toe, down the stairway again," wrote Sarah. "We could hear him coming every time. We despised him." Always listening on the stairs, forcing them to eat those tough lamb chops when he knew they were vegetarians; plotting behind their backs, spreading those lies: the old ladies have lost the power to function, the old ladies can't hold it any more. "And that cornball speech," wrote Sarah. "Huck Finn, Moby Dick, and the six o'clock weather report all rolled into one. Inspired no doubt by the lap, lap of the waves as he drives to work each morning through the tunnel under the Hudson River. And he wonders why he was always the vice."

They had charted the good voyage, he said. They had paid the toll and set the ship of state on the right course.

They could trust the steering to others now. But only to the wise and brave navigator. For the seas were rough. The lights were flickering. Larboard the great ships were swishing by. Starboard the small craft were edging closer and closer. There must be no rushing ahead; no falling behind. One small mistake and the waters would engulf them. His respectful proposal to the good ladies was: fasten their life preservers, for the harbor was hidden in the haze. Disembark to that safe shore they had so richly won. Elect a new captain, someone whom they could trust, someone who had sustained them in their black and hungry hours before the mast.

The old ladies regarded him, stone-faced. And how about the mainsail and the topsail? How about the spinnaker that it was well known little old ladies liked to jump over at night in their nor'westers and tennis shoes?

Pardon them, please, while they leaned over the hatch and puked.

To be more explicit, said the vice-president, beginning to worry (why were they looking at him like that?), "There is no need even to go outside the building for a new Leader. Why do you not then choose someone from the great Invincible complex?"

"Why not?" said the old ladies, cagey. Who did this pussyfooting simp think owned Invincible now anyway —except 2,989,642 old ladies? What did he think they did down at Wall Street—watch the pigeons flutter? Did he actually think they'd overthrown the previous govern-

207

ment for the doubtful privilege of sitting again on those
overrated standpipes, shaking their legs and waving their
canes like nuts? Had he forgotten the fate of the treach-
erous pigeon Randall? Did he not recall the last survey
of that other clown, the consultant from M.I.T? "Never
underestimate anything whatsoever about an old lady."

Laughing themselves silly (just wait till the next stock-
holders' meeting), they did as he asked. They elected
someone from Invincible, a natural: the President. Other
things on their mind now, they did not much care who
was Head.

Marjorie Jo was eager to try out her new step—a kind
of Bach-bend-shove, on the street corners. She had decided to pretend he had not come at all. HE HAD NOT
COME—at least up on the West Side of New York City.

Sarah, busy composing those government decrees—
"Down with the Computer, Bring Back the Human Race"
—missed the friendly write-and-answer spirit of her Advice Column. When the letter arrived from Mr. Epstein,
whose wife had earlier left his bed and board after a
tense, ungrammatical exchange, she was delighted.

"Here I am, as you suggested," wrote Mr. Epstein
one day from his farm. "Had to come to Colorado to
find the right kind, but like it fine. Remembered what
you said about your childhood, showing the prize products in the bank window, immense pride, huge crowds,
and all that sort of thing. Mine are undoubtedly a livelier
breed than yours. One knocked out the window of the

bank and leaped over the banker, an unpleasant Western type. But am sending you two samples from the farm as agreed."

"What is that damn noise downstairs?" asked the new Head, the president of Invincible, the next day. "Is that an antelope I hear down there?"

"There is no noise downstairs," said the vice-president, still wondering. How had he failed? He had worked like hell on that speech. "We're repairing the bottom drawers, that's all."

"Sounds like a lot of mad antelopes jumping around to me," said the Head, and a great fear came over him. At night he would think he heard antelopes jumping behind him, trying to get his little battery.

"We've got to get rid of these antelopes," he told the people. "Look at 'em leaping there. They're dangerous. The baby in that pouch may be holding a machine gun." "The antelope has no pouch," said those who had been to Tree Top House in Kenya, an overnight stop where they had watched the animals go by; travelers, they knew a thing or two. "You are thinking of the kangaroo, the marsupial," they said.

But the Head took it to the people. "How about it, are there pouches on those antelopes or not?" And he flashed his little electric battery. My goodness, thought the people, watch that thing light up. They were impressed. At last we have a Leader with a good-sized knot on his head, they thought. A Head with a head, for a change. "Looking at it from here," they said, "we can see that there are definitely pouches on the antelopes." And they decided to sew some on.

"They could take over the city with those pouches," said the Head, the Leader. "Remember the old ladies and the pigeons—how they took over the city with those shopping bags?"

He sent out the decree: Get rid of them.

There were protests. Why, some of our best friends—. Look, have you tried the steak? Listen, which one did he mean? With those shopping bags and those pouches it's pretty hard to tell. Why, it's easy as can be. The antelopes have four legs and when they sit on the standpipes their horns point backward.

Don't everybody's? asked someone.

But she was just a little girl youth of America and the next day all the antelopes were rounded up and banished.

Safe at last, the Leader turned off his little battery and looked out over New City. A peaceful quiet sat on the half towers. Nothing stirred above or below. At first. Then high on the wall out there something moved. Small at first, no taller than a standpipe, no deeper than a shopping bag, no wider than a wingspread. Gradually it grew bigger and bigger, closer and closer. He turned on his battery; red flashed in the air. Danger. He focused his long-lens binoculars. Invincible. He waited. His knot began to throb. The light from his battery flared once and went out. But he had seen enough.

CHAPTER NINETEEN

"To anyone watching, we must have seemed a strange procession," wrote Sarah, in domicile again. "First, as befitting her position, came an old lady on a slope leading an antelope with a pigeon in its pouch. Following, in a protective attitude, rode a little girl youth of America in a new small domestic car. Behind her, at a respectful distance, walked Sister Mary Magdalena, in all the glory of her technology. Next came the bearer of the beer and the Bible, then that other indispensable sustainer of life, the one called the Great Tit. Bringing up the rear was our pentecostal nut with the flag and the sign: He Had Not Come to New City, Either.

"So we returned, as we always shall. If we are unable to walk we will link hands and inch along. When this is no longer possible we will crawl. But we *shall* return—we *will* fight on! How could we stay away when the world is so great and the things to do so wonderful—so many fresh walls to cover, so many new doors to open?

"How could we ever give up?"

The Portrait

Though Mrs. Payne's interest in the portrait had certainly waned, Blanche still did not believe she had forgotten it. Delighted the day Mrs. Payne telephoned and invited her to go to the museum, she waited in vain for some word of another sitting.

"Mr. Payne's not having the AAs this week, thank goodness," said Mrs. Payne, "and it would just be a great privilege and joy for me if you'd go to the Met with me. Excuse me a minute, Blanche." There was quiet on the wire then and Blanche thought Mrs. Payne must have seen a bird through the window; a new chickadee or something must have flown up to the feeder, she thought, and smiled to herself at the picture of her friend dashing from the phone, dodging the arthritic Airedale so she could stand at the kitchen door and welcome the little stranger bird to the feeder. When still the phone remained silent she thought that perhaps Mrs. Payne had rushed on past the feeder to chase off another hunter; it had been a hunter who interrupted the portrait painting. Then in a few moments the friendly, warm voice came again on the wire, saying something nice, as usual. "Also they have a big restaurant with fountains, and I want you to be my guest for lunch."

"Why, Mrs. Payne," said Blanche, and knew now that Mrs. Payne had been busy counting her money. All that ice cream and cake for the AA bunch kept her stripped.

She had not worked steady for Mrs. Payne for some months, as Mrs. Carruthers, a wealthy Morristown lady, had asked for all her time and Mrs. Payne had insisted she go, but the Paynes' place, in a wooded Jersey area where acreage had been comparatively cheap when the Paynes first married, was not too far from Blanche's apartment in town, and the two friends kept in touch over the phone. Before the frequent visits of the AAs the white woman, no longer young, had taken a course at the Art Students League in New York. All her life she had longed to be an artist, to paint. "Every letter I'd write on that old typewriter in town, beating off my paws all those years we were saving up, I'd think, Artist, artist, why aren't you an artist?" Her eyes, blind blue, flamed into Blanche's. "Mrs. Payne, you *are* an artist," said Blanche. The passion of the other, usually so shy and reserved, worried her. "The nudes in the living room and the pictures of George Washington prove it." The nudes, it was true, were not finished, lacking in grave particulars, as Mrs. Payne had missed class those days, and parts of George Washington, the Airedale, were just dubbed in, like haze, but to Blanche the over-all effect was lovely. "Your whole home shows you are a real artist."

Mrs. Payne, after consulting many books from the public library and paying exorbitant fines for overtime, had designed the brick cottage called Dutch style, and coming up the country lane, bordered with lawns of daffodils in spring and white daisies in summer, lively with birds and squirrels, chipmunks and rabbits in all seasons, Blanche had thought a hundred times, My friend Mrs. Payne, the artist, lives here. Childless like Blanche, and without close neighbors or friends, Mrs. Payne, since Mr. Payne now worked early and late at the office, recouping finances wasted in the pre-AA days, depended much upon the companionship of George Washington, her feathered friends, and her art, and with her, Blanche thought, enjoyed perhaps her deepest personal friendship. Though Blanche had lived alone since her husband's death, her sister Eunice and her bowling friends came by daily for a quick beer, and this kept Blanche company; she often thought Mrs. Payne was lonesome. Mr. Payne now slept on the porch with George Washington and on the nights the AAs came allowed him to stay in the room with them, enjoying the coffee and cake and the testimonials. But Mrs. Payne would go sit in the old Chevrolet and watch the stars.

On Saturday afternoons when Mr. Payne and George Washington looked at the football games on the TV in the living room, Mrs. Payne, artist, listened to the opera on the old radio in the kitchen, alone. "Maybe you should back down a little on the artist deal, Mrs. Payne. Give up

Milton Cross and have a sneak drink instead with the boys inside." But Blanche never said this, like she also never said, "Mrs. Payne, pardon the intrusion, but if you didn't spend all that money on birdseed, you could get the old washing machine fixed and we wouldn't have to stoop so at the sink."

The most she could ever bring herself to say in the way of advice or faint reproof was "Mrs. Payne, you should get out and bowl when the AAs come."

They had finished their afternoon coffee under the trees (Mrs. Payne did everything she could outdoors, though the light hurt her eyes and she wore a sunbonnet for their protection) and were lazing and watching the birds the way they liked to. "It ain't exactly outdoors but Eunice and me belong to a nice bowling club." "I couldn't bowl if they put the goal post in my lap," said Mrs. Payne. "Besides, I'd rather paint." And she had set Blanche down on the bench by a plate of figs and begun her portrait. That was how Blanche loved to end her day with Mrs. Payne, out there painting. As some people performed best with music on the side, or a quart, Mrs. Payne responded best to figs; they had been in her girlhood home in the South and were now bought at some expense from the local groceryman, a smart Italian who on the nights the AAs came also made a killing on the ice cream and cake. "Hold it just that way, Blanche," said Mrs. Payne. "That's just perfect." Blanche, leaning forward, her hands dropped, looked hard at the feeder. A chipmunk, using soft feet, slipped up behind the chickadees and stole their suet. Blanche almost laughed, but remembered in time and held her lips stiff.

"Blanche, I believe this is going to be the best thing I've done," said Mrs. Payne, stepping back from the canvas. "I'm excited as I can be about this." Catching the excitement, Blanche had run over to view the portrait. "I believe you can make the skin darker," she said after a moment. This was not in the nature of criticism; she was merely giving Mrs. Payne license to darken the paint, a kind of brown-gray, for she suspected that some delicacy, a refinement in Mrs. Payne, had kept her from painting her that black right in front of her. "I ain't that light-complected," she said. "You know now they say black is beautiful."

"Now, Blanche, in that famous art class I took I was noted for my skin tones." Laughing, Mrs. Payne passed the figs to Blanche, who peeled one and gazed at the canvas. Pleased as she was with the portrait, she had been surprised she looked quite that way, thinking of herself as different, not better-looking, but different-looking. From North Carolina, she had a trace of Cherokee in her and it had surprised her to see Mrs. Payne had found it and put it on the canvas. "Are my cheekbones that high?" It was her opinion that the portrait looked more like her sister Eunice (squarer than she, though a better bowler) and this made her ask, "Mrs. Payne, are you sure that's me?" Her eyes had come out kind of slant, headed down toward the nose, but her hair was pulled back, neat.

Mrs. Payne sat down by the figs. "You know, Blanche, it won't be exactly as you know yourself from the mirror, or from what you feel yourself to be. It'll be as I see you. Me." Full of fun, she pounded her chest and pretended to knock herself off the bench. But she caught the figs. "Me, the famous artist."

"I can't lose on that," said Blanche, satisfied, and Mrs. Payne, swishing her behind in her shorts and squinting her eyes under the sunbonnet like a put-on artist might act, waiting to get the right dab, flecked her brush over the easel again. Blanche leaned forward on the bench and resumed her pose. "I'm ready, Rembrandt," she called. Years ago Mrs. Payne had taken her to Princeton to see the Charles Laughton movie and she had never forgotten the name. Now in the richness of her expectancy over the portrait, and the memory of that happy trip, smiling with Mrs. Payne in Princeton, she used the name again. "Get going there, Rembrandt," and Mrs. Payne prissed up to the canvas.

The birds had seen the hunter first, scattering in fearful flight, then the chipmunk, then George Washington, who rose, creaking, to greet him as he came on down the path through the woods. Stunned at his nerve, Mrs. Payne stood speechless; she herself had painted the No Trespassing signs posted at all entrances to the property.

Mrs. Payne did not believe in killing any little living thing except roaches. Now as the man came on into the clearing by the feeder, she started toward him, swinging the easel. "Kindly take that gun and get out of here as quickly as you can." "Just doing a little shooting—" The man let his free hand rest on the Airedale's head; George Washington licked it. "We shoot nothing on our place except hunters," said Mrs. Payne. "So get out." "Well, for God's sake." The man appealed to Blanche. "Get off the grounds like Mrs. Payne says," said Blanche. "Can't you see them little birds is scared? Can't you see we're painting a portrait?"

That had finished the painting for the day. Mrs. Payne had packed the paints back in the old whiskey box that said 90 Proof and shoved it in the hall closet. But that evening when Eunice and her friends came by for a quick beer, pre-bowling, Blanche told them of the portrait. "You'll get it tomorrow." Eunice set the date, almost a challenge. "Ain't gonna take long to finish it off, if it's just to the waist. Unless she's stalling." "'Course she's not stalling," said Blanche, and the next day called up Mrs. Payne on the phone. "Mrs. Carruthers has conked out on me today. You want me to come for a sitting?" But Mrs. Payne was still upset over the hunter. If there was anything Mrs. Payne hated more than hunters it was the new highway and the subdivision developments that had ruined the hill where she and Mr. Payne went to see the sunsets and watch the deer. Blanche had to

call Mrs. Carruthers and tell her she could make it after
all. Eunice gave her five more days. "Tuesday then. Unless she's just putting that old southern blah over on
you." Eunice had had some bad experiences with her
madams and did not understand anybody as refined as
Mrs. Payne. Blanche thought that was a shame and took
a second beer, something she rarely did. The following
day she called again, ready to say, "How my portrait
coming, Rembrandt? Have I got any prettier?" But there
was no answer on the phone; George Washington's arthritis had flared up where he had licked the hunter's
hand, and Mrs. Payne had taken him to the vet for a
checkup. Tuesday when Blanche appeared on her regular work day Mrs. Payne had already set up a rented
sewing machine.

"The AAs are coming tonight, Blanche," she said, and
they had stitched new curtains, the old ones were all
washed out from the frequent meetings. Mrs. Payne
wanted to keep Mr. Payne happy in the AAs; whenever
somebody else fell off the wagon or fell down on the enter-
taining she wanted him to feel like saying, "Well, hell,
we'll be glad to have you at our house then. Any time."
"We were just there last week." "What's the difference?
We're all in this together, aren't we?" When the new
curtains were up and the sewers were having their afternoon coffee under the trees, Blanche said, "Have we got
time for a short sitting before I go home? A quickie, as
Eunice says?" Mr. Payne had built a trellis to shade the

feeder and for a moment Mrs. Payne watched the chipmunk slide down the vine to the cool seed. Then she
shook her head. "Sorry, Blanche, but I've got to paint the
kitchen floor again." She kept the flat paint near the
kitchen steps, ready to mix when she got the AA signal.
"They practically live in the kitchen, you know."

"Bye, bye, blackbird," said Eunice when she heard of
this latest postponement, and in the following months,
though pride kept Blanche from mentioning the portrait
to Mrs. Payne (she felt that Mrs. Payne should be the
first to bring up the subject), it, along with Mrs. Payne,
had become the butt of many jokes among Blanche's
friends. "Ain't Mrs. Payne the one gonna paint your portrait, Blanche? Ain't she that famous French painter Suze
Anne we heard so much about?"

And they would wink among themselves and grow sly.

"Ain't she the one wear the little Abercrombie Fitch
sunbonnet, Blanche? 'Cause it resembles a little sunbonnet she done wore down in dear old Dixie when she
eating all them figs?"

"That's my girl," said Blanche and did not remind
them of Mrs. Payne's eye trouble. It was an old-fashioned, protective feeling she had for Mrs. Payne, a feeling
unpopular now, she knew, and subject to ridicule among
Eunice and the bowlers. But Blanche had it, anyway,
and though she did not flaunt it, as they said in the ads,
she did not feel that she had to apologize for it, either,
and often tried to give Mrs. Payne little things she

needed around the house, things that had worn out or got shabby and were too expensive for Mrs. Payne to lay out the money for now. Like a hose Blanche had bought at auction or a spray gun so Mrs. Payne wouldn't have to bend her back so when she painted the kitchen floor. "That's my friend, all right."

"You gonna wear the sunbonnet in the portrait, Blanche? You don't want to catch no suntan, you know, 'cause I imagine you done turned up a bit gray in that portrait. I imagine all your teeth is fallen out by now, it taken so long."

"I imagine I still have a good skin tone," said Blanche. "I imagine my skin tone is still okay. In many ways the skin tone is quite the most important part of the picture."

"Yeah, if it old Whitey's," said Eunice. "Ain't Mrs. Payne the one who fed the mouse, Blanche? Ever' time it come out from under the refrigerator she have a drink of warm milk and nice piece of cheese ready? Purely Grade A that is, of course."

"I'm glad she done it," said Blanche. "She don't slight nobody."

"Well, look to me like Suze Anne off painting a portrait of the little mouse instead of you. I bet she painting the little mouse in the sunbonnet. I bet the title say Come to Abercrombie When the Sun Is Shining Bright." And they would open more beer. "Be sure and call us when the portrait is ready. We'll bring the beer, mousie bring the cheese, and we'll have what they call a hanging of the portrait."

Blanche let them talk on, for of these, her girl friends, none had ever had her portrait painted and few had been to the museum, though their children had.

The day before the trip to the Met she let her sister know about it on the phone. "Eunice, don't you all come by tomorrow," she said. "I won't be here. I'm going to the Met with Mrs. Payne."

On the other end of the wire she heard Eunice set down her beer can. "What Met is that?" asked Eunice. "The ball game?"

"The Metropolitan," said Blanche. "The paintings."

"Going to pick out the portrait, huh?"

"Can't ever tell," said Blanche. "We're gonna have lunch in that big fancy restaurant with the fountains."

Eunice popped another can; she kept a spare by the phone, down near the Yellow Pages, so she didn't waste that time just talking. "You better take your overshoes along then," advised Eunice. "In case old Whitey knock you in the water. And something to bring the portrait home in. Don't mess up the skin tone."

Blanche hung up. The next day Mrs. Payne came by for her in the old Chevrolet and together they rode to the Madison station where they parked the car.

"Blanche, I asked you to come with me," said Mrs. Payne when they were safely on the train to Hoboken (doctoring the rose geraniums with ashes and manure

water, Mrs. Payne had lost track of time and they had
rushed up the steps of the train just before it pulled out
of the station), "not because I think I know any more
about it than you do." She looked at Blanche; she would
not force her opinion on anybody; she respected everybody that much. Except hunters. "It's because I can't
think of any greater joy than to show this wonderful
whole new world to somebody for the first time."

"Mrs. Payne, of course you know more about it than
me," said Blanche. "I don't know nothing. I'm ashamed
of myself for not having been before, too. When I've been
so close to this great privilege and not taking advantage
of it." She smiled at the other. "Now, though, I'm glad
I waited for my guide."

"I am too," said Mrs. Payne. "I just hope you like it as
much as I do. The minute I step in that big downstairs
hall I feel transported. I get a lift that carries me right
through the next AA meeting."

They laughed over this and Blanche said, "I bet I feel
the same way. I bet I get the same lift." She already felt
enchanted and meant to get the lift or bust.

"What I thought we'd do," said Mrs. Payne, "if it's all
right with you, is instead of trying to take in the whole
thing at once, we'd just work at one section, a special
exhibit. Later I hope we'll come back often."

"Anything you do suits me," said Blanche. "Even this
train ride's a big treat to me." When she and Eunice went
anywhere they just got on the bus or hopped in Eunice's

sporty Chrysler and shot the gas to it. For fear now that
Mrs. Payne, holding up her end of the conversation,
would ask what make of car Eunice had, she diverted
her attention to the window. "Look out there," she said,
and pointed away from the highway. "Ain't that a fig
tree in that yard?"

"It surely is." Mrs. Payne clutched her arm. "Look, I
see some little figs on it. Look quick."

Blanche looked and though she could not see the figs
she said she could, the way she did when they watched
for the deers. "Did you see that deer, Blanche, back of
the tree there?" "Sure I saw him." That was the way she
was going to do it at the museum, too; not be a gump
like Eunice. When she and Eunice had gone to Atlantic
City all Eunice had done was gump. Old Whitey cheating
us on the gas price. No, it don't remind me of when we
was little girls. It reminds me of a big fat Jew city. All
right, gump, she had wanted to say to Eunice, what you
gonna gump about next? But they had been in Eunice's
car, the Chrysler.

"Mrs. Payne," she said suddenly, "how's your little
mouse?"

Mrs. Payne ducked her head, laughing. "You remember my little mouse?"

"Sure I do. Me and Eunice talks about it often. How
you fed it by the refrigerator and left the saucer of water
for it, and kept old George Washington from hurting it."
After the AAs had been there the little mouse came out

to get the cake crumbs. "When I get lonesome I always think about Mrs. Payne's little mouse." Blanche smoothed out her skirt and patted her gloves; her hat wasn't much, just one of those prong things you clap on and it sticks, but her purse and her summer suit were good.

"Blanche, you make me look like a hick," said Mrs. Payne.

"Why, Mrs. Payne, you got on your stylish little Abercrombie Thai silk." Mrs. Payne always dressed well, in the best clothes, but she did it on sales and, instead of the sunbonnet today, wore a cute brim hat from Peck's.

"I haven't got your pretty skin tone, though," she said, and they got off the train at Hoboken. "Now for the tubes," said Mrs. Payne, "then hi, ho, Blanche, only two more means of conveyance and we'll be there."

Stepping at last into the great domed hall of the museum, Mrs. Payne, watching her anxiously for her reaction, said, "Doesn't all this give you a lift? Do you feel it like I do?"

"I should say I do. I feel that lift coming on," said Blanche, and started to enter a large room.

Mrs. Payne stopped her. "That's just the bookstore, Blanche. Where you can buy the reproductions if you see anything upstairs you like. The real paintings are upstairs." Turning then from the reproductions and prints, she followed Mrs. Payne to the elevator and the rooms of the special exhibit. A few groups here split up, everybody on his own, but Blanche stuck close to Mrs. Payne. Once, though, she thought Mrs. Payne was through looking and she strolled on ahead, but Mrs. Payne wasn't quite ready, there was something about the last picture she hadn't settled yet, some way the paint was spattered, and Blanche hurried on back. She didn't do that again. Some of the paintings seemed strange to her, of unnatural subjects, cupid boys and fat ladies that kept her silent and shy in their presence, but Mrs. Payne, able to sense it, soon led her on to the more familiar.

Here was a plate of figs and pears by a blue pitcher (or were they figs and pears? wondered Blanche, looking again. What kind of a pitcher was that?), a mountaintop by her friend Suze Anne, a windmill by her pal Rembrandt, and Blanche lingered here, hoping for some mention of the portrait (in the Princeton movie Charles Laughton had painted portrait after portrait, mostly of himself), but Mrs. Payne went on to an old shack by the beach that reminded Blanche of the house where she and Eunice as little girls had lived in the hot summers with their grandfather. Each day they had played in the water, hopping the waves and shouting, while their grandfather, a freed slave, had stood on the shore, owning the sea.

Three colored people, an older man and two girls, a nice family, decided Blanche with quick pride, were looking at the next picture when she and Mrs. Payne came up. The man indicated points of interest in the picture, like an artist would, lifting his finger but not too high, getting near the canvas but never touching it, and one of the girls turned, laughing, and said, "A rose is a rose is a rose." Cued by Mrs. Payne, Blanche laughed with the rest, till the others, smiling, walked on so she and Mrs. Payne could take their place in front of the picture.

I've seen this picture before, thought Blanche at once. "Mrs. Payne, haven't I seen this picture before?"

"You probably have," said Mrs. Payne. "It's a favorite of mine, and I know they have reproductions of it."

"Have you got a reproduction?" said Blanche.

"No, I don't think so."

"Maybe I saw it at Mrs. Carruthers'," said Blanche, sure she had not (picture of a bridge table was more Mrs. Carruthers' speed), and she stepped on with Mrs. Payne. When she looked back another group was around the picture, shutting off her view.

At lunchtime, the handsome restaurant (the striking black and white décor, the white canopy, the airy gilt chandeliers) gave her a momentary feeling of uneasiness, until across the pool, past the boy-fountains like Leaping Lenas, she spotted the family she and Mrs. Payne had chummed with. Warmed by a nod of recognition from one of the girls and softened with memories of her girlhood summers, before Eunice had become such a gump, she relaxed. "Mrs. Payne, this is all just lovely," she said. "Eating here with you in all this beauty. Getting all this lift." When she got home she meant to blow it up to Eunice and the girls (she would omit the fact that the restaurant was cafeteria style and that she had chosen a cheeseburger) but by now she had stolen a fast look in the mirror of her purse and knew what she had to do before she went home. Her chance came after they had finished lunch and were leaving the museum. Mrs. Payne stopped at a booth in the big hall to pick up a lecture program.

"Mrs. Payne, if you'll excuse me while you're busy with your program, I'll step into the store here just a minute."

Knowing her friend was too polite to follow her, she hurried into the bookstore. The glass counters were crowded with post cards and pictures, reproductions that sold at fifty cents or a dollar, but there was none of the picture she had seen upstairs. It was not a face one could forget; when she looked at it upstairs it had seemed almost like a little bell had rung to get her attention, but she thought it had been because it was lunchtime. Now she went the length of the narrow room, looking on both sides, darting from counter to counter.

"This one?" said the saleswoman when she found it at last. "By Picasso?"

"That's me," said Blanche. "That's my girl." And full of lift, and the relief of finding the picture (it was stuck on one of those racks that you turned, like a fan), she went back to Mrs. Payne. "Got something for Eunice," she explained, the big envelope tucked under her arm.

But Mrs. Payne was preoccupied with her own thought

now. "Blanche," she said, "you remember that portrait we started that day?"

Blanche shifted the envelope to her other hand and pulled on her glove.

"Yes, I remember it," she said. "I think of it every once in a while."

"Well, being with you here today has been such an inspiration to me I'm going to get it out of the closet next week and work on it." Then she added, half laughing, "If the AAs don't get me first."

"Why, Mrs. Payne," said Blanche, aware that through no fault of Mrs. Payne she would never get the portrait. If it wasn't the AAs it would be something else, the rose geraniums, George Washington's arthritis, or the highway that would eventually come plowing through Mrs. Payne's kitchen, scattering the ice cream and the cake eaters, scaring the little mousie, and changing Mrs. Payne's whole life, even Princeton. During the train ride home, sitting on the side where the figs showed, away from the highway, she thought of what she was going to tell her friend when they parted at Madison.

"A rose is a rose is a rose, Mrs. Payne," she called after the old Chevrolet. The white woman, not understanding, but smiling anyway, drove on into the Jersey traffic. Across the street Blanche could see the sporty Chrysler already parked, and, clasping the envelope, she went in to try to pass off her portrait of Gertrude Stein on Eunice and the girls.

The Traveler

" 'You got a hell of a hump on your back there, lady,' Doc told me. 'I may have to cut it off. Where'd you get that thing, anyway?' 'God's great gift, Doc,' I said. " 'And I ain't helped it none crawling up under the house after all them stranded dogs and cats.' "

Stopping at a gate in the country hills, she made this her opening, explaining: "People let 'em out on the highway, you know, figure they'll lose the direction and can't get back home. Try to fool 'em, get out a minute and stretch, like they gonna stay with 'em, then they jump back in the car. 'Drive on quick,' they say. Or 'Goddam it, I can't, he's looking right at me.' I've seen some leave drinking water in a bucket lid so that years afterward, when it woke 'em up at night, they could tell themselves, 'You left the drinking water in the lid. Turn over and sleep. He had the drinking water.' But drinking water ain't what them poor little abandons need. They come creeping up to my open gate or hide under the house and I have to crawl up and pull 'em out to pet 'em, to make 'em feel like they wanted again. Hence the Hump, as I heard a fellow sing on the TV. Didn't go down on the bass like you'd naturally expect for a hump. Sang kind of a high C, more like it'd suit a conniption."

Traveling, she had made it her custom to mention the hump first, to put people at their ease, and now, her hand on the closed gate, she waited. On the porch of the flat-roofed frame house an old man sprawled by an uncorked jug. In the yard a younger man was passing out biscuits and yams to a cluster of ready children. Watching, hoping for refreshment to come her way, Emma smiled at the smallest boy, who almost offered his biscuit, then, gazing solemnly at the mountains, ate it himself. She pulled back her hand.

"I ain't never turned one away yet. Cats, dogs, whatever. One time I found a little idiot child stumbling and crying in the dark where they'd put him out. He'd got too much for 'em to handle at home, I guess. Or maybe there were other kids in the family it didn't seem fair to. He's the only one I ever lost, just died right there on me, flopping his little hands. I had good luck with all the puppies, but I can't forget that one little simple child I lost. Seemed to hump me up more than ever. Miss Gloria was the first one to notice it. 'Has something terrible happened?' she wrote. 'Your flap measurement has shot way up.'"

She paused again, watching the food pass from hand to hand. When the boy got his potato he seemed to consider, then, eating it, almost smiled. This time she had kept her hand at her side.

"You see, some people say a hump ain't good for a thing, get rid of that hump, it don't make your dresses neat. But one of the nicest relationships I ever had come out of this contact with Miss Gloria. She's the lady I send to that makes the dresses with the little extra flap for the hump to fit in. Happened to see it advertised in the back of the paper. Try Our Little Cushion Flaps. And I said to my husband, 'You think I should get one, Mr. Ellis?' 'Sure,' he said. 'It might cover up the damn thing.' So I sent in my measurements and struck up a nice corre- spondence with this lady that sews my flap in. Some of the other sewers, thinking about the coffee break or pay- day, leave a needle in or put the flap in backward. Just don't give a darn. But Miss Gloria always sews it in just right, with a cute message. 'Hi, there, good-looking' or 'Happy everything, dear.' Once she wrote, 'Strike a blow for women's rights.' Took up half the flap. 'Send me your picture,' I wrote back, 'so I can see how such a nice lady looks.' She sewed back in, 'Oh, you don't want to see my picture. My hair ain't so good no more.' I imagine she teases it in front, more to hide where it's got thin than for style. Mr. Ellis thought she might be bald-headed."

Thinking of Miss Gloria's message when Mr. Ellis had finally died ("Congratulations, dear. Now you can travel. Now's your chance to exchange your fine outlook on life for a view of the world. Now's your chance to use that great potential"), Emma fingered the latch of the gate. "So when the last little pet was gone I put my things in this sack, closed it with this rope one poor little puppy had tied around him, strapped my old quilt to my back, and lit out," she said. "I swap teaching for victuals. Fried, dried, cooked, or raw."

"Where's your books?" asked the man, and did not lift the latch.

She was used to this one. Over in her home county they had made it hot for her. "Where's your degree?" they asked. "You can't fool us, you can't hardly write your name. Don't know nothing except what you hear on them TV programs. Listening to them damn sunrise college courses with all them dogs yapping in your lap and sitting on your hump." That meant she had not yet traveled far enough from home, so she had put a county or two behind her before she tried it again. "You ever hear of Socrates and Plato?" she asked now, bringing in the big names on the sunrise lessons. "They never had a book on the place. Walked back and forth the livelong day, gabbing. Never did sit. Sure, they had to lie down sometimes, dead drunk, but they had these pretty young fellows they'd taught to prop 'em up. Never missed a word, either."

"What can *you* teach?" asked the man, and opened the gate now. On the porch the children lined up by the old man and waited to learn.

"How about the alphabet to start off with? How would you like to learn to make an A, kids?"

"Show her," said the father, and the kids, using sticks

to draw in the hard ground of the yard, made As the shape of the mountains in the distance, with the growth of pines between the slanting lines for a crossbar. The littlest shot his crossbar out to the side, a porch, a rest; a kind of show-off, he would always do it differently, add something for others or for himself, to get in the limelight.

"Ain't that the goddamnedest biggest A you ever saw?" said the father. "Ain't a airplane up there that can't see it. What else can you teach?"

"How about an O?" said Emma, skipping to a letter she hoped was not yet known here. "How would you like to learn to make an O, kids, the shape of the world?"

"Show her," ordered the man, and the kids, looking out to the blue mountain lake for a model, made Os. The boy, restive, secretive, shaded his O where the shadows from the trees had already hit the water. The boat anchored near the trot line came out interesting, sort of like the hump on the traveler's back. Flattered—or was the little bastard challenging her?—she looked at him, trying to get something going with him, for the O making was evidently of a high quality here.

"Listen, lady, my kids' pictures have been in ever A- and O-making magazine in the country," said the man. "Show her how they take your pictures, kids." And the kids, as though posing for the camera, put on airish, educated looks, and lined up again by the old man.

"Yeah, you got the prize with the A and the O, all

right," admitted Emma. "But how about the Alcibiades Act? Can these kids prop up a drunk and keep him talking? Do they know the proper tilt for a toper?"

"Show her, son." And on the side of the porch, the little A maker, moving with all the skill and the grace of the Greek boys, propped up the old man, his arms free to lift the jug, his tongue loose, the proper way.

Beaten now, Emma walked, hungry, down the steep path. Once she stopped and waved back at the little A maker, who came a few steps after her, with biscuit and yams for the road. Then he ran back and she saw him bent over in the yard, making fun of her hump for the others.

In the town a roadside stand was selling Folksong Kits, Guitar Guides, How to Play the Five-String Banjo and the Spanish Guitar plus 100 Simple Folksongs. "Big Sing in the Next City," said leaflets tacked to the stand. Emma had been pretty good at humming around the house, improvising about a sick puppy or the old Greek drunks, and when she read further, "Cash Prize for Best Original Song," she decided to enter the contest. Traveling, even on foot, cost more than she'd expected; handouts had been disappointing, and her learning and fine outlook on life so far unappreciated. "Sing and You Can Make It," Miss Gloria had sewed into one of the flaps and now Emma, turning the pages of the songbook, got the hang of it, not hard, and went on her way. Singing free and easy, as she had not for a long time ("Stop that bellowing like a bull," Mr. Ellis had always yelled, "I'm listening to the ball game"), she passed on through the town, practicing. She passed by houses with people resting on the porches or outside under the trees, sipping, living this rich life with paper napkins and folding tables for all. In one yard a young woman, wearing a large hat with veil, and a long-sleeved dress and gloves, was picking figs.

Emma watched her a moment, enjoying the picture, then went into the yard. "Can I help you with those figs?"

The woman studied her from the tree. "Well, somebody sure can," she said. "I'm so darn hot I'm about to die, but I have to wear this rigging or I'd swell up like a fool from this fig milk."

"Come on down," said Emma. "I'm not allergic, as they say on the TV."

"Boy, I sure am," said the woman. " 'Take care of that pretty skin, though,' said my husband. 'I don't want to see my best girl all popped out like a Memphis whore.' He's one of them southern big shot talkers, you know. Been to Congress and spoke at a nigger thing once. Phony liberal. Thinks he's it."

Emma climbed the tree, careful of the limber branches. Leaning against a limb and clutching the bucket between her knees, she picked with both hands in a rhythm like milking. As she delicately balanced the weight of the hump against the bucket of figs, she imagined herself to be a tightrope artist, her childhood dream. "See the great dancer, folks," she cried. "See Emma, the bareback rider, right this way." Holding out the bucket of figs recklessly, she almost fell. The woman below looked away, embarrassed, but tickled, too. When Emma filled a bucket with the ripe fruit and passed it down, the woman, getting into the spirit of it, would hand her another, with the flourish of a ballet queen. When at last Emma climbed down from the tree the two caught hands a moment and giggled, sharing. Then Emma got a bucketful for the road.

She stood off, looking at the bucket. "I ain't seen one of these in some time. This is a old-timy syrup bucket." In the tree she had been too busy to notice.

"Hell, except for the phony liberal deal, we're old-timy people," said the woman. "But personally I think we should progress with the times. Like you," she said, and came to the gate with Emma. "You know, I ain't ever seen a person with a hump that their dress fit so neat. It's all right for me to mention it, ain't it? I mean you ain't sensitive about it, are you?"

"Excuse me," said Emma. "I got so taken away with the good time and the figs I forgot my company manners. You don't have to feel sorry about the hump, hon. It's just some of me that didn't fit in the mold right. Part of the crossbar that came out extra. Seeing it makes people glad they ain't me. So I figure it's doing a little good in the world. It helps people and it don't hurt me."

"You sure got a nice outlook on life about it," said the

woman. "I imagine it ain't so easy carrying it around, though.

"Oh, it ain't that hard," said Emma. "Sure, sometimes I feel sort of dragged out and low, but I figure that's because I'm human, not because of the hump. Of course, when I was a little girl I had some bad times with the other kids making fun of it. Cried my eyes out about it. Then I found out it come in good in fights. I could swing it around and knock 'em out before they knew what hit 'em. They run home yapping, 'Emma hit me with the hump, Mama. Emma ain't fighting fair.' That's what you call utilizing your infirmities, hon. Putting your potential to work, is what a good friend of mine wrote me. 'Get in there with that grand potential and fight. That thing is just loaded with potential.'"

"Pardon me, may I ask if you're married?"

"Yeah, hon, even a humpback can get married if they're determined. What give me the most trouble was getting the first beau. I had to do all sorts of things I ain't telling about to convince him he wasn't gonna lose out on nothing. But I expect you had to turn an extra trick or two with them liberals so to speak, didn't you?"

"Boy, you can say that," said the woman. "But I was noticing your dress when you was in the tree, dancing around like that. I thought, My goodness, that sure is a cute idea for a hump. Here's one lady that sure ain't set down and let things pass her by."

"I got a special lady that tends to my dresses," said Emma, pleased. "Miss Gloria, if you ever need her."

"Heavens, my husband would never let me get a hump." But she wrote down Miss Gloria's name. "Your children all grown, the reason you out on the road?" she asked.

"I'm childless, hon, sorry to say," said Emma. "Something about Mr. Ellis didn't work out just right. Some little hitch somewhere. How about you?"

"Oh, I ain't got *that* trouble," said the woman, studying Emma. "You have this nice big frame, though. I wonder. Maybe it's the hump," she said, then stopped. "Look, I got no reason in the wide world to think that. And I sure ain't got no business saying so."

"That's all right, hon. That's what he said, too: 'The hump is in the way.' And he turned against me. You see, I think he was always sort of ashamed of it, like it was a reflection on him—a man who couldn't get nobody but a big old ugly woman with a hump."

"You ain't that ugly," said the woman. "You carry yourself so well."

"Well, he didn't think so. In the end, like so many, he was just a mean old man."

"Liberal hell," said the woman.

"But I don't want you to think I been lonesome, hon. I've had my pets, and the poor little soul I lost. Then Miss Gloria's just been a real big thing in my life. And I have my TV lessons. I been around some, too, not so much lately as when I was younger and had just come out of the mountains." She looked at the woman proudly. "I ain't meaning to brag, hon, but I bet I'm the only old lady you ever saw that peed in the TVA."

"My goodness," said the woman. "You sure don't look it."

"Oh yes, I had quite a little fame in my time. But it wears off and people forget. And that was in the Roosevelt administration, of course," said Emma. "Not that that detracts one bit from the feat. Soon after they went up on the rates." And she was still a moment, carried back, remembering the roaring dams, the sluices open, and the great mountains around, smoky and beautiful, and the others, girls then, giggling, daring her on, and it not easy, either, not allowed with the hump. But she had been determined, kind of like the little A maker, to have her moment in the limelight. She had lost track of the girls now but something about the experience had always endeared the President to her. "He believed in the four freedoms, you know. I believe in the fifth. Of course Mr. Ellis always said Roosevelt was a Jew boy. Seemed to have it in for him and Miss Gloria. Couldn't bear for me to have any nice friends."

"The type is not unusual," said the woman, and walked back of Emma to take a further look, though in a delicate manner and lost in thought.

"Mr. Ellis said it ain't slanted right," said Emma.

"They sure can't downgrade you on your flap, though,"

said the woman. "Where you gonna sleep tonight?" she asked. "I'll bed down on this quilt somewhere," said Emma. "Find me a little nook somewhere and hit the hay." "If that Congress bunch wasn't coming to free-load again I'd ask you to stay here so we could talk some." "I'll be all right," said Emma. "Ain't nobody gonna bother an old lady with a hump. If they do they'll get the surprise of their life."

They waved good-by now and Emma went on her way. She ate some of the figs and, when she was far enough away, sold the others. Along the road she found some rocks and ran one on the rope through a hole in the empty fig bucket. With this she made a kind of accompaniment to her singing, jiggling it in her hand to keep the time and set the tinkle. Though she walked slowly, pulling her hump up for comfort, the flap was beginning to rub her back and she had to stop and rest. "How about one of our little fur-lined flaps then?" wrote Miss Gloria once. "I don't believe in killing little animals any more than you do, but it would certainly be nice for the hump."

Emma placed a cool green leaf under the flap ("No, thank you, dear, live and let live") and, adjusting the quilt, walked on, gazing up at the cars as they passed, but no one offered her a ride. One carful of boys yelled, "Let's shoot the old lady's hump off," and they pretended to fire guns, "Pop, pop, pop," but she ducked, carrying on the joke, if it were one, and the boys drove on, laughing. Nobody stopped for her, though now she stood close to the road and shook the rock in the bucket, calling attention to her presence. Lots of cars, she noticed, had dogs in them, sniffing the breeze, and when a terrier, business bound, ran down the road toward her, she scooped him up expertly, tripping him with the syrup bucket and holding him, careful, the way she had learned under the house.

"I'm traveling to the city with my sick little dog," she said when a car finally stopped.

"Unfortunately we ain't headed there," said the woman. "But Lord, you can't walk all that way. I told my husband, 'For goodness' sake, let's stop for that old lady with the hump.' Pardon me for calling your attention to it," she said.

"I done heard the news, hon," said Emma. "Now I got to get my little dog to a doctor. See how restless he is."

"He ain't foaming at the mouth, is he?"

"No, the poor thing is just weak."

"Ain't you got a bought piece of leather to lead him on in the city?"

"Just this rope," she said.

"Well, hop in. We'll take you part of the way."

She held back nicely. "I ain't taking you out of your way none?"

"Why, of course not. We just glad to."

In the back seat she held her hand over the little dog's mouth. "You know," she told the woman, "you

THE TRAVELER

remind me of a good friend of mine. Miss Gloria. Something about the way you do your hair so becoming."

"Well, thank *you*," said the woman. "Ain't you nice to say so."

"You so much like her, so kind and thoughtful," said Emma. "Helped me so much." ("Get in there and make that thing work for you," Miss Gloria had sewed in the flap.)

The woman asked her husband: "We can take them on further, can't we, Daddy?"

"The dog looks mad," said the man.

"He ain't mad," said the woman. "He's just sick. Holy smoke," she said. "Ain't you ever looked sick? Ain't you ever looked mad?"

"Boy, that old woman is sure playing us for suckers," he said. "She's got that dog trained to play sick. I ain't surprised she'd got something stuffed up her dress to make that hump. And look at that rock and rope she's carrying. She's liable to hit us on the head, strangle us both, then cover us up with that quilt."

"Why do you distrust people so?" said his wife. "Just tell me that, please. Every time I try to do something nice, like stop for somebody with a hump or something, you ruin it. Mama taught me to trust people."

"Mama, Mama, Mama, Mama, Mama, Mama. Goddam it." And he stepped on the gas.

They put her out in the middle of town. The little dog gave her an outraged look before he started for

250

home, a long ways off; once he stopped in indignation and barked back at her. Then, never good at directions, he set out again, not even sure where he'd come from. Signs led Emma to the square where under the trees people were lined up to register for the contest. "Where's your guitar?" asked the boy when her time came. "I don't need a guitar," she said. "I'm a rope rock singer." "I ain't got it written down here," he said. "You ain't likely to," she answered. "I'm the original." On the benches she sat apart from the other singers, watching.

The convicts, Fatty Bread Jones and Lancelot Lee, sang first, for they had to get back to the pen, and they had a pure, plaintive tone. The blind played next, followed by the deaf, singing loud but in key, their own, then Crip Smith, celebrated in that section, and followed by Hernia Higgins, or Old Truss to the trade. Listening, Emma soon found out that after the announcement of the title, which could also be the main body of the song, repeated after a preliminary strum, other words of the song were unimportant or non-existent. One chord and several words did it. Some of the songs made little sense and were not intended to, but some touched her. "No Skulls Are Handsome," sang a young man in the late afternoon. "Viet Nam" and "Draft Card Blues" followed.

When Emma's turn came she faced a tired, noisy audience. Pulling the rope for time, she stood in the singers' circle. "Prop Him up Proper, Alcibiades," was her first choice and she made it peppy, a kind of a jig.

Remembering how graceful the little A maker had been propping up the drunk, how like a dancer when, stooping and mincing, he had made fun of her, she shook the hump as she rattled the rock in the bucket. This proved to be popular and in a more pretentious vein, hymn style, she rendered "Run out the Crossbar, Run out the Crossbar, Help Somebody Today." This was a dud and, building up to her prize song, she sang next "Figs, or A Bucketful for the Road," and some listeners thought she said "Pigs" and not "Bucket" and shouted rowdy approval. "Phony Liberal" was a pace changer and a direct lead into "TVA," niced up, with fake waterfall accompaniment. Then it was time for the big one. A real performer, she stepped back, tilted her head, wet her lips, and stepped forward, presenting the title. "Just Flopped His Little Hands and Went."

Before she could open on the fine high note she thought appropriate, she saw them coming through the crowd.

"Here's the old lady," said the man. "She beat this little dog with a rope with a rock on it. We found him just now, running around in circles, not knowing where he was."

Emma stood, silent, her hands still clasped, as in prayer, or shelling peas.

"See, there it is," said the man. "Look at that big rock. She was in our car with this sick dog. The poor thing was foaming at the mouth where she'd beat him."

"We don't *know* she beat him," said the woman.

"What the hell's that got to do with?" said the man. "I didn't like her from the start."

"Well, she had that big hump though," said the woman. "I sure am glad I ain't her."

"Watch out," the man called. "She's fixing to throw that rock."

The singers crowded around her now and though most of them did not believe she beat the dog, or cared, one warned, "You better move on, lady. We don't beat dogs here." "Just people," said somebody. Funny, this was repeated for laughs. "Hey, lady, have you beat any babies today with that rock and rope?"

Emma packed her rock and rope in the bag with the syrup bucket. The little dog trotted ahead of her, trying, twice in one day, to find his way back home. Emma watched him. You dickens, she thought, and when he turned once more, raised her hand, and he ran. At a corner of the square she thought the man and the woman passed her in the car but nobody spoke. In some ways the woman's husband reminded her of Mr. Ellis, mean —he was the one finally put up the barbed wire to keep out the little lost ones—to the end.

"You don't need all these damn dresses," Mr. Ellis had said, "just to get that message on the flap. That lady is using you. Keeps sending these messages to keep you buying the dresses. She and that damn crooked Roosevelt are going to put us in the poorhouse. Just order the flap next time." This had seemed cheap to her, a poor response to Miss Gloria's free, friendly way, but when a letter had come, regretting that the flap could not be sold without the dress, a union regulation, Mr. Ellis had been triumphant. "Some damn little Jew man like your pal Roosevelt has got in the flap business and making a racket out of it," he said. "They're doing it with machines."

It had been hard to believe that no nice lady had sat there, hair teased to hide the thinning part (not too noticeable, but it ran in the family), pins in mouth, needle threaded, sewing in the message, hoping to hit it off just right: "Viva la Hump," "Chin up on the Anniversary of the Little Lost One." How had the tiny needles, punching, jabbing, made their lies on the flap look so human?

"They did it with the damn new flap duplicator," said Mr. Ellis. "Invincible Company makes it."

But, to Emma, Miss Gloria was as real as the one other person who would haunt her always. "My goodness, Mr. Ellis," she had called that night. "Come on out of the house quick and help me with the little fellow." "Well, get your damn slanting hump out of the way so I can see." Sick, sucking on her skirt like it was his mother, the little soul had died, though, right there on the highway.

Leaving the town now, she started on her travels again. Sometimes she saw her shadow, ugly against the trees, and she would stumble on the path. Then remembering her high potential—Hon, you ain't thought of half the ways to use it yet—she would straighten up and walk on, headed somewhere to help with the hump.

Oh, Pity the Dwarf's Butt

The old man and the rooster hit it off with Elizabeth at once. She fixed up the back room for them with a Belgian rug from Woolworth's, plus a dresser and bed, good, but discarded when Jess got the new job in the liquor store, and Mr. Lloyd, the old man, put up the window shades. While the crippled rooster perched nearby Elizabeth served morning coffee and toasted biscuits, or she would make Mr. Lloyd his favorite, spoon bread, surprising him sometimes with bits of real ham they still sent her from the country. Jess was busy at the store and Carol, thirteen, had quickly found a friend, but Elizabeth, too proud to push, was often lonely since they'd moved to town. Planning treats for the old man and the rooster gave her special pleasure.

Sometimes Carol, toe-dancing in from a dentist appointment or a briefing session with her friend, Janet Halliday, would find her mother and the rooster, a balding Plymouth Rock, keeping each other company in the yard. In his youth in Detroit Mr. Lloyd had done some bantamweight boxing, and on the days he volunteered to teach this skill to the Boy Scouts and at the Y, Elizabeth entertained the rooster, calling him by name, Jack Johnson, and wheeling him about the yard to admire some special flower their pal had planted. The old man, a former apartment superintendent, loved the yard. After years of basements and boiler rooms, of homes that were never home, he could not get enough of working in the yard, digging and discovering, planting and pruning, and, in order for his pet more comfortably to share his great delight, had made the portable rooster stand.

Of salvaged, sidewalk oak, the stand stood bed-high. Three steps, linoleum-carpeted and measured meticulously to the old rooster's reach, led up to the landing. A strip of bathroom marble, rescued from recent rubble, covered the landing with an elegant air of antiquity. The perching rod, one easy hop back, was a sawed-off chair rung. Parallel to the rod ran a padded prop for the crippled wing. A chute funneled the droppings to a trough. Linked by string to the prop, a signal bell added a gay, exciting note as if the moment the engineer jangled the bell the stand would take off on its rollers for some daffy cuckoo land.

In very hot or very cold weather the rooster was allowed to stay in the room and the old man would shake ashes on the droppings, piled like sculpture in the trough. "My God," said Jess, "get that old man out of here with that rooster," but Elizabeth said, "We don't mind a few ashes, do we, Jack Johnson?" After the old man went to the hospital she began talking more and more to the rooster. "Perk up those droopy feathers there, our pardner's gonna pull through," she assured him. Or "Don't worry, I been handling Jess for twenty years." Every day she pulled up the shades and aired the old man's bedclothes and fluffed his quilt. She had given him the wedding ring design; close as he'd ever got to the real thing, she told Carol. Too sweet or too fast on his feet, he had evaded the real thing. Respecting his privacy, she had never inquired why. Carol had learned this respect too, and knocked when she went to his room and was polite to the rooster. The day the bad news came from the hospital her mother folded up the bedclothes in an act so final that Carol, teetering awkwardly on ballet slippers, a gift from the old man, wept. The rooster crouched low on the stand, head extended, as if now he must appear wise, something bigger than he had been, an owl, an eagle. Or get the ax.

"Leave the rooster in or let him out?" asked Carol.

"Let the rooster decide," said her mother. "It's just a pity he didn't have a chance to tell his friend good-by."

Mr. Lloyd's body was to remain at the funeral parlor to await the arrival of his closest kin, two California nieces (the third, lately in a car accident, was unable to come), and when on the busy day of the funeral no one else from the family was free to sit with the old man, Carol said, "Well, I'm going."

"Why, hon, folks are getting away from that practice now, viewing the body," said her mother. "Don't anybody want you to see 'em all laid out and can't talk back. It ain't fair."

"I'm not gonna say anything to him. I'm just gonna think about him."

"Are you, precious? I think that's sweet." Usually she liked the old ways best but when they moved to town everything had been Episcopalian, faddish. "Dress pretty in your white pleated jumper," she said, and went in to handle Jess. Carol, searching for a suitable box, could hear them from her room.

"After all, the Lodge is paying for the private interment, and we won't be out anything, except a few incidentals at the hospital," said Elizabeth. "Candy I took the nurses now and then. A few phone calls, I guess."

"Yeah, two long-distance calls to California," said Jess.

"I imagine the girls'll pay for 'em when they come. I want to ask 'em back here after the church service. Give 'em a chance to relax and have a bite before they go back to California. That's a long trip, come and go the same day."

"I guess that's the reason they never asked the old man and the rooster to come live with 'em," said Jess. "Felt a delicacy in asking the old rooster to take such a long trip."

"Mr. Lloyd wouldn't have gone to live with 'em if they'd asked him," said Elizabeth.

"Or else they heard about us being the sucker type,"

said Jess. "Taking in all the homeless old men and roosters in town when nobody else would."

"Listen, their sister's sick and they got to go back the same day. And we gonna have something nice for 'em," said Elizabeth. "Shrimp salad."

"Shrimp is expensive," said Jess.

"Yeah, they punk to peel, too. But we gonna have 'em. With those little hard sesame rolls and use the Limoges china. So bring home some of that nice white wine from the store. We'll use the crystal glasses."

"You don't think just 'cause I work there I can bring that stuff home free, do you?"

"Bring that white French kind with the hard-to-say name."

"I think a nice domestic do just as well."

"I don't want something cheap you're pushing at the store. I want the imported. Three or four bottles will do it, I think."

"Hell, it ain't no wake, is it?"

"No, but I want to show how much we thought of Mr. Lloyd. We're his family, and I got a new way to do eggplant. Bake it whole, then scoop it out into hot olive oil."

Carol, who would never be as light on her feet as the old man had been, tiptoed past her parents' room.

"Step in the doorway a minute, baby," called her mother. "Let's see how pretty you look." Carol walked on, faster. "I look all right." The lid of the box flopped but she held it with her hand. "Wait a minute. Papa'll drive you down in the car." "I can take the bus." She was at the foot of the stairs now, out of sight. "All right, Papa and I'll go on directly to the church then. Be careful on the bus, though, precious. Don't speak to anybody." "My God, Elizabeth," said Jess. "The kid takes the bus to school every day. Leave the worry to the drivers. They ain't been drinking any four-dollar-a-bottle wine."

They were still talking when Carol slipped past the kitchen door and, knocking first, entered Mr. Lloyd's room.

Two blocks from the bus stop, the funeral parlor beckoned her with an electric arrow. No one met her in the tiny office, more of a window with a slot than an office, then an attendant looked at her through the slot. "I've come to sit with Mr. Lloyd," she said. The eyes behind the slot stared at her; Janet Halliday had showed her how to throw out her chest and tighten her skirt, even pleats, after she left home. "You alone?" "The others are coming later." "Is that flowers for the deceased in that box?" She kept her hand over the lid. "No, sir."

Meeting a person, Carol always noticed their teeth first, did they have to wear braces like she did, were they better or worse than hers. Janet Halliday always noticed their sex, were they men or boys, and was taking a census to sell the State Department later. The attendant came around the side of the window now to lead her inside and for the first time Carol really saw him. Knot-nosed, he had a skinny young head with as much of the modern hair as the parlor would permit, and a long lower lip that would give him trouble when he got his first dentures. Unless he sucks in first, then puts the powder in, thought Carol, who had made an extensive study of the subject Teeth. Or he could just let them dry, then suck, like her father did, she thought. He was young enough to enjoy being called "sir" and when he wasn't wearing the black suit wore Levis, she thought— probably without drawers.

"No, sir," she said again, saddened for the moment, knowing about the teeth and the hard time ahead for him. (Never free from the fear that they might fall out in front of everybody. Making love one night with this specially beautiful girl, it might happen. "My goodness," she would say, "what's that extra noise? Sounded like false teeth falling out.")

She had not expected the parlor to look so bare; she had pictured it as more like a dentist's office, mean but clean with a place to spit. In front of a curtain, like a stage, was a long table and here, highlighted by two electric candles and the cross of white carnations her family had sent, lay the remains of Mr. Lloyd, that good old man. On either side of the coffin, stands from the church and the Lodge bore testimonials of flowers and banners. A middle aisle divided three rows of chairs. When business was slack they played bingo here, thought Carol, or came up from the embalming room for a cool Coke.

The boy left her and, holding the lid of her box slightly open, she stood by the coffin. Mr. Lloyd's teeth had been very bad, worse than hers. He'd had a malocclusion, suffered in the ring, he'd never been able to get fixed. Root canal work, too. A dentist said he put in a gold post and all he put in was a paper clip. But even this had not made him bitter and, looking down at him now, Carol could imagine him, stylish, prancing around the ring, toes pointed like a dancer's, the paper clip, not yet rusty, gleaming in the bright lights as he bowed to the roaring crowd.

Her lips trembling over the braces, she turned away. A muffled sound shook the box in her hands and, pressing down the lid, she sat close to the aisle; she meant to stay until the boy came back. Once when she heard a noise in the office she pulled the pleated skirt tighter and reared up, chesty, holding her breath. Janet Halliday, whose parents for business reasons had all their teeth and Janet's capped, knew just how to tell if they had on no drawers. "Just stand off and look to the side," she said. "Grab your chance when opportunity knocks, for God's sake. Stick out them pattycake breasts and forget the teeth hangup. Quit crying over the weak and the underdogs and get your mind on the important things of life. Make me this census report."

Breathless, Carol now waited. But it was only two women outside in the entrance; she let the air go and, deflated, listened to them.

"If it hurts that bad, let's get a doctor," said one. "Bound to be a doctor tied in with the funeral parlor somewhere." "You know I don't let no doctor fool around with me except Dr. Hunnicutt," said the other. "Honest though, Agnes, you'd think we ain't used to taxis in California, the way you go slamming doors on people's fingers." "Listen, Rose," said Agnes, patiently, thought Carol (like her mother trying to explain the rooster to Jess), but with some fire, too (like when Jess said the rooster had to go), "I was just waiting back to pay the fare like I did at the airport. How did I know you were gonna hop out first again and stick your finger where the door shuts? That don't mean you got to holler about it all day. One time Mama got out of the car with Sister driving and without looking back Sister slammed the door and drove on down the street, Mama running alongside the car, her finger caught in the door. Mama didn't make the fuss you have."

"Hush the hero-worship about Mama and come on," said Rose, and the two women followed the boy into the room. Carol jerked up again, ready. "Left or right," said Janet Halliday. "Just keep your eye on the ball."

"Jesus, a bat's flying in my face!" said the woman called Rose, and too late Carol realized that when she breathed up, sexy, the lid of the box had flown open. Feathers filled the air; a frightened old bird banged his wing against a chair. But before his astonished audience could move he flapped forward, gained wind, and in a cloud of speckled glory, landed on the coffin. In sweet, piercing farewell, he crowed. His homage done, he then meekly submitted to the box.

"Now I've seen it all," said Rose. "They don't even have no roosters at funerals in California."

"They have the singing canaries," said Agnes, a small, intense woman with teeth like a picket fence. "Puff out their little chests and sing so pretty. And last year I saw a baby elephant. His skin was bad. Man with him kept pushing him till I thought, Don't push that baby elephant like that. I would have bought that little elephant from him right there but John said wait till Billy Dee gets married and we have the spare room."

"Yeah, you've seen the canaries and the elephant," said Rose. "And by now the riderless horse is old stuff. But have you ever seen a rooster?"

"I saw the traveling dwarfs," said Agnes. "Hired. They lined up on each side of the grave like they gonna hoist the casket. They worked hard, lifting, kind of scrooched down like frogs. But stronger men had to do it in the end."

"So you saw the dwarfs," said Rose. "Get 'em in a fight,

they mean as the devil. Jump up as high as they can, cheating, and get a uppercut on you."

"You should have seen the miserable look in one of them poor little fellow's eyes when he found out he wasn't going to make it with the casket," said Agnes.

Carol held down the lid of the box, sick about it. "Maybe he had his feet spraddled too far apart," she said.

"No, the feet was just right," said Agnes. "I watched it too many times."

"Then you gonna have to quit going to all them free funerals till they get some bigger dwarfs," Rose broke in impatiently. "In the meantime, hon, we feel honored with this rooster. Your folks don't know you brought him, I bet." Rose, the bossy, cross woman with the too short skirt and the too large legs, smiled. A gap between her two upper central incisors, a crowned porcelain on the left and a screwed-in acrylic on the right, gave her a childlike, persuasive air, and when she said, "Come on with us in a taxi, hon. If the subject comes up we'll tell your mama the box with the rooster is our luggage," it was tacitly agreed that the four would keep this event of the rooster to themselves, that they would leave out Elizabeth particularly, for no reason at all. It was accepted that the funeral service at the church could now be only second best, an anticlimax, that the benediction, the final gesture, had been delivered here.

Carol stood to one side of the boy while he tied down

the lid of the box. A feather had caught on his coat; she picked it off and he grinned up at her. The future was plain. Suck, and still they might not stay in; this could go on all their lives. Even when she lay there in his arms he would go chopping his teeth like that. "Sounds like false teeth hitting the mattress," she would say. Or perhaps she would pretend she did not hear them at all.

The nieces paused at the coffin. "Don't Uncle look nice?" said Agnes.

"He looks peaked as hell," said Rose.

Some people had the modern service, scarcely mentioning the deceased's name and skipping the Lord's altogether; instead of the Bible a poem by a favorite author was read, and if it were by one of the better-known poets the reader would go adenoidal, nasalizing the non-commitment. Elizabeth wanted the Lord in hers; she didn't want to have to look in the paper next day to see at whose funeral she'd been, either. Mr. Lloyd's service, with testimonials from his Bible class and his Lodge, should have met her requirements. There were Scriptures and hymns. The Boy Scouts formed an honor guard and passed in review. A eulogy proclaimed the old man's generosity and unselfish service to the community. But, sitting beside her mother in the church, Carol saw her mouth a silent "Amen," then withdraw to the corner of the pew, left out somehow. When the band from the Y hit the shrill notes in "Taps" she leaned forward as though expecting to soar to some high sorrow but instead bowed her head, excluded, alone. On the front row, the nieces, involved in some private pain, sat like strangers.

Carol, concluding her census on the Boy Scouts, cried briefly and began on the band.

On the day the old man had had the stroke in the flower bed Elizabeth had carried him in her arms to his room. After the service she showed the nieces the room. "Come out, Jack Johnson. Come meet your visitors," she called. The nieces waited, and from the rooster, hunched by the door where they had deposited him before the church service, there was no sign of recognition. "So which one of you lucky ladies inherits the old rooster?" asked Jess. "I guess the rooster be happier here," said Rose. "They ain't no travelers, you know." Looking around his room, she sought a more portable memento of her uncle. "The rug's a fake and the quilt passes to my daughter. The boxing gloves and the tool chest go to the Y boys," said Elizabeth. Since the nieces had not bothered to see him in many years or supplement his meager income, it was her expectation that they choose small things—a pipe, a wallet. But Rose, a shot of medicinal bourbon having temporarily dulled the pain in her finger, walked about the sun-filled room as though so long a trip for the funeral of an old man, hardly remembered, deserved a larger bonus.

She stopped at one of the windows. "Who put these shades up so straight?" she asked. "Did Uncle cut them shades that good?" Elizabeth nodded and Rose, blinking in the sun, pulled cautiously at a shade. "Look at that, smooth as can be," she said, impressed. "Dr. Hunnicutt hung all my shades and he ain't measured one single pole the right length. Always had to patch it out with a extra piece of wood. Then you scared to touch it. 'Measure it like you do the bones,' I told him." She smiled and Carol watched the two front teeth. "'It ain't the same at all,' he said. 'Cutting the bones is quite different. The ends don't have to match.'" "The shades go with the room," said Elizabeth, and Rose strolled on toward the bed. "This thing over here would make a nice momento. What is it?"

There was a moment's silence. "That's the rooster stand," said Elizabeth.

The short legs walked like an appraiser's to the back of the stand. "Just as neat as Sears Roebuck," said Rose after a while. "With these little stairsteps and the marble-top privy." "Got a bell on it, too," said Agnes, getting interested. "In case he woke up at night, his wing aching or the light in his eyes, or he thinking about something that upset him that day and he want to tell his pal about it. He just ring the bell. That give me a idea for the elephant room. Though I'd have to raise the shaft some and make the string stronger, I could do it," she said with conviction.

"Yes, sir, that's really a nice little old rooster break-front." Rose stood off, admiring the stand. "Antique it up, put running water in the privy, and it'll be worth money someday. My friend, Dr. Hunnicutt, collects quite a few antiques."

"I'll say he do," said Agnes, but Rose, pretending not to hear, came to the rooster stand again, studying it so closely that Elizabeth, suddenly uneasy, led the way quickly from the room. "Come on in to lunch," she said.

Lunch, laid out buffet style on the glass table, was served on the side porch overlooking the beds of pansies and phlox where the old man, graceful as an aging deer, had loved to work. "Look at all these pretty little flowers. Ain't they sweet?" said Agnes. "Dr. Hunnicutt grows glads and a great big peony," said Rose. "Make such a handsome bouquet." "Your uncle liked the smaller flowers," said Elizabeth. "Kept stooping and weeding and digging, even when he shouldn't. I'd call out to him, 'You and Jack Johnson come on in for our treat.'" Passing out the Madeira napkins, her hands trembled. "'Lead him on in, Jack Johnson,' I'd say."

Rose sank into a cushioned chair. "We were sorry we couldn't ever get Uncle out to take a ride through the redwoods with us. But it's such a long ways off." "Yeah, Cal's a long ways off," said Jess, and left it in the air: even with the night rates. He brought in the wine cooler. The visitors took note: one bottle. "Look, the rooster's come in the yard to join us," said Rose, and seeing the single bottle, missing Dr. Hunnicutt, she added wickedly, "I believe he wants to go back to California with us. I guess me and Agnes could take him off your hands. Put him in a box." "Make some air holes first, though," said Agnes. "Run a pole through it for him to stand on."

"He's looking for his old friend," said Elizabeth, jabbing butter into the sesame rolls. "Ain't he losing a few feathers on that wing, though?" Rose said, and smiled knowingly at Carol. But Carol, listening, watching, no longer knew her. "It's an old injury," said Elizabeth, looking at the rooster as if she were no longer certain. "That's how your uncle found him. Crippled in the road, run over." "I just mean he's kind of trailing it there in the dirt." "That's peat moss," said Elizabeth. "Your uncle bought it to protect the little early-blooming plants." "I didn't mean anything uncomplimentary," said Rose and, glancing at her watch, settled back in the chair. "I think the wing's very becoming at that angle." She held up her glass, signaling Agnes: Say something about the wing. The plane's not even scheduled to leave for five hours. "In fact," said Agnes, "the wing's my favorite piece of chicken." Rose shot her a warning look and she added, "Though I ain't proud of it, naturally. The organ of flight. I prefer shrimp. But them little shrimp has a hard time of it, too, skittering around with their heads cut off."

Carol, imagining the shrimp swimming upstream, trying to make it back home, the baby shrimp paddling alongside their mothers, crying, "Mama, Mama, where is your head?" turned from the dish, stricken. "Mama, why didn't you have spoon bread for Mr. Lloyd?" she said. Elizabeth looked from Agnes to her daughter. "It don't go with the shrimp," she said shortly. "The eggplant goes better." Carol, like a secretive peach, rose on her toes and said no more. "This eggplant's delicious, isn't it, Agnes?" said Rose. "Dr. Hunnicutt serves it with his drinks. Kind of a stand-up dunk." "I like eggplant just about any old way you fix it," said Agnes, prodded. "When we were kids, though, we wouldn't even pick 'em out of the patch. Lay there on the vine, blaring up braggy, 'Pick me, pick me, look how big I am.' But we wouldn't do it. We showed our independence on the eggplant." Lay off the downgrading of the eggplant, said Rose's indignant look. We got to stay here till 7 P.M. "The wine ain't bad neither." Rose held up the glass to the light. "In this beautiful thin crystal. It's even very light on my poor finger old Agnes here smashed in the taxi."

"Look," said Agnes, "Mama'd be there yet, running alongside the car, if they hadn't hit a red light, and she didn't grunt like you have about that finger."

"The car was probably falling to pieces. The latch was loose," said Rose. "Sister ain't had a decent car in her life."

"Sister's got one of them Volvos," Agnes said. "Sister's got a nice car."

"Sister had a nice car," corrected Rose, and Agnes, reminded why they were hurrying back home, was silenced.

Carol, hoping to escape unnoticed, edged on her toes toward the door. Elizabeth's sharp voice called her back. "Not yet, young lady," she said. "Pass the rolls." Silent then, Elizabeth sat apart from the nieces. "I mean the wing's dragging a bit, that's all. I think it's rather attractive that way," said Rose, and took a roll. "Ain't these little rolls nice and crisp?" Carol, the plate extended, pointed the crisper of the rolls toward Rose and stood before her, guessing. Which would it be? The crowned one on the left? Or the screwed-in acrylic?

Rose chose the intended roll and settled in again. "Yes, sir, I'd have given anything when I was a little girl to have a rooster stand with stairsteps." She motioned past Carol to Agnes: Say something about the rooster stand.

"Maybe the old antique collector'll give you one," said Agnes, tired of the orders: Brag on the eggplant, nix on the chicken wing, low-rate the funerals. Carol looked at her, thinking of the dwarf, squatting, his butt sprung out like a baseball batter's, tears in his eyes when he could not hoist the coffin. Spraddling her feet, she squatted a moment, pushing up, trying it. "Watch that plate," said Elizabeth. Carol turned her eyes back to Rose and waited.

"Wonder how much of a boxer Uncle really was," said Rose. "I got a friend, Dr. Hunnicutt, follows the fights." Smiling, thinking of something far off, she bit into the roll.

"Oh, he was just a amateur dabbler," said Jess. "I doubt if he ever even made the paper."

High on her toes, Carol watched her mother. Champion of rooster rights and rebuttal time for the dead, possessor of a rare supernumerary lower incisor, Elizabeth jumped to her feet. "He didn't give a damn about making a two-bit newspaper," she said. "He cared about keeping the kids off the street. He cared about giving 'em lessons in boxing and carpentry so they could amount to something. He didn't stand around counting bottles. He helped people. That's the kind of an amateur and dabbler he was."

Jess looked at her. "So the second funeral service is over," he said after a moment and the nieces laughed, embarrassed. Elizabeth strode to the porch's edge. "Amen out there, Jack Johnson," she called. "Look, he knows you," said Rose. "Sure he knows me," said Elizabeth, rejoining her guests. "He's a regular member of the family."

"That's what our uncle wrote us," said Rose. "'This is my family now,' he said. 'I hope you girls understand that and realize why I must decline the invitation to live with you in Cal.' There are lot of the aged there, you know. Old ladies come in by the bus loads." She shifted the half-eaten roll to her uninjured hand. "Yeah," she said. "I'm gonna think about them stairsteps a long time.

And the marble-topped privy. That's something I won't ever forget, even back home with all my friends." Now she looked down at the shattered crust in her hand, at the twisted gold crown sparkling in the sesame, and with a grand gesture—Up your shade pole, Dr. Hunnicutt—swallowed the rest of the hundred-dollar roll.

Disappointed, Carol turned away. She had bet on the acrylic.

"Please excuse our daughter now," said Elizabeth. "She has to report to Janet, her girl friend, who's been so sweet to show her the ropes since we came to town."

Released, Carol started upstairs. Intrigued with the teeth, she had completely forgotten to take the census for Janet Halliday. Of the fifteen Boy Scouts nine had weak labials, four wore braces like hers, and in five the mandibulars had undershot the maxillars to an almost apelike degree. The boys from the Y had come off better; three were good and only seven in a dreadful state, with stains; six had the telltale Hutchison incisors and would have to take the cure. All of their occlusions were terrible. But only the boy from the funeral parlor was set for early dentures. Even when she lay with him under the wedding ring quilt his teeth would probably go suck, suck. "Well, take them out first," she would finally say, knowing that always he would be too proud to do it. Unless she took off her braces, too. See, I am as naked as you.

Weeping now for the world, for the orphan shrimp,

for the dwarfs with their pitiful little butts (push and tug and never make it), for the eggplants begging to be pulled (Look how small I am where I'm stuck on the stem. I got my weak points, too), she heard the voices from the porch.

"By the way," said Rose, "we'd like to pay you for the phone calls to California."

"Heavens no, it's nothing," said Elizabeth.

"Yeah, nothing's too expensive for your uncle's funeral," said Jess.

Carol waited on the stairs. Spraddle more, then get a knee under it would do it, she bet. Or if they were strong enough, clamp your teeth on a rope tied to the handles and pull up.

Then she heard her mother's voice again, "There's plenty more wine, of course," and went on up the stairs.